Your Old Pal, Al

HG

Your Old Pal,

By Constance C. Greene

A YEARLING BOOK

Published by
Dell Publishing Co., Inc.
1 Dag Hammarskjold Plaza
New York, New York 10017

Yearling ® TM 913705, Dell Publishing Co., Inc.

ISBN: 0-440-49862-7

Reprinted by arrangement with
The Viking Press (Viking Penguin, Inc.)
Printed in the United States of America

Second Dell printing—April 1982

CW

To my old pal, Donna Ireland

Your Old Pal, Al

chapter one.

"I'm not getting any younger," Al said.

"Who is?" I asked.

"I've got miles to go before I sleep, and I seem to be standing still." I noticed that underneath her new tweed jacket she was wearing her old brown vest, a sure sign she's in the pits.

"How come you're wearing that"—I pointed to the vest—"when today is practically boiling?"

"False summer," Al said, looking critically at the sky as if she could see a weather report there. "We always have a false summer just before school closes. Pay no attention. We'll have a relapse, I guarantee."

Suddenly she hissed through her teeth, "Listen,

I'm pushing fourteen, and once you're fourteen, it seems *something* should've happened to you. Something memorable."

"What'd you expect?"

Al lifted her shoulders until they almost touched her ears. "I don't know. I might find out I was a missing heiress. Or maybe the illegitimate daughter of a French count. Or I might be discovered by a TV tycoon." She dropped her books to the sidewalk.

"There I am, sitting, enjoying a sausage-and-pepper pizza, minding my own business." She bent her knees to show she was sitting at a counter, enjoying her pizza. "And along comes this TV tycoon in a three-piece suit, with his hair all styled and everything, and he takes one look at me and says, 'Pardon me, miss, but if I may say so, you're precisely the type we've been combing the city for.'

"Then he decides to star me in his new sitcom, which turns out to be a romance with a lot of laughs, an unbeatable combination, and it also turns out to be the hit of the century.

"Well"—Al smiled ruefully at herself—"maybe not of the century but of the half century. But it's big, really big. I am able to buy a mansion for my mother and also a Mercedes-Benz, on account of this sitcom runs in prime time and takes the Nielsen ratings by storm. I'm on the cover of *Time* and even *Newsweek* . . ."

A little old lady walking with a cane came up behind us. "You're blocking the sidewalk," she said. "Please step aside."

"I'm a TV star," Al told her, "in the process of being discovered," and she stepped aside.

The little old lady drew back as if she smelled something bad. "In this world," she said, "you meet all kinds. Life is not what it used to be." She tottered off down the street, shaking her head, muttering to herself.

"I made her day," Al said. "She thinks I'm on drugs." She bent and picked up her books and went on talking.

"And people would stop me on the street and say, 'Aren't you Laura in *Squat Down in Squalor*?' or whatever. I think that'd be cool. That and all the residuals."

Here we go again.

"What are the residuals?" I said. Al frequently uses words I don't understand. One nice thing about her, though. She never says, "What! You never heard of residuals!" or anything like that. She doesn't treat me as if I were a total idiot because I don't know the meaning of a word, and I know plenty of people who do that.

"Money, baby." Al did a little tap dance. "That's all. The folding green stuff. Every time they show your sitcom on reruns in the summer, especially if it's in prime time, they have to fork over big bucks. Which are otherwise known as residuals. Which will make you rich. You savvy?"

I savvied.

"You could always write a book that they'd turn into a major motion picture for six figures," I said. "That's a good way to get rich quick."

"I'd settle for one they'd make into a minor motion picture for five figures," she told me. "I'm up for an ice cream cone. How about you?"

"I'm broke," I said. Sometimes, when I say, "I'm broke," I feel like a record that's gotten stuck.

"Then we'll share." There was an ice cream cart at the corner. "One mocha chip cone, please," she told the man. "First this year. How's business?"

"Stinks," he said. "You want small, medium, or large?"

"I want large but this is all I have," Al said, holding out her money. "I guess I'll have to settle for small, huh?"

"You must be psychic, lady," he said.

Al looked at me. "L-A-D-Y," she mouthed.

"Have a weird day," she told him when he handed her the cone.

"I already did," he answered.

"If that guy ever broke down and smiled," she said as we walked away, "he'd probably bust a gut."

We stood waiting for the bus. The branches of the trees lining the street stretched spidery little tentacles rimmed with leaves toward the sun. They were trying hard. Maybe they'd make it.

"Did you ever think about living in the country?" I asked Al. "Instead of here, I mean?"

"I have," Al said casually. "Once, when my mother and I were trying to decide whether we should move East, we rented a little house outside of L.A. We had an orange tree in our backyard."

"An orange tree? In your own backyard?" I couldn't believe what I was hearing. "Why didn't you ever tell me that? That's absolutely fabulous. Did you pick oranges off it?"

Al shrugged. "Sure. They were sour, though. We also had a walnut tree."

"With real walnuts growing on it?" How did she take things like this so calmly?

"It wasn't so much," Al said. "I'd rather live here. It's much more exciting. Have a lick."

"You first. It's your cone," I said. I couldn't get over having an orange tree plus a walnut tree in your backyard. I'd never lived anyplace that was different. Up to now I'd had a fairly boring existence.

First she took a lick, then me. It was delicious. The sun really was hot. We had to work fast.

With her tongue, Al pushed the ice cream down so nothing stuck up. It was all inside.

"It lasts longer that way," she said.

"I think Vi's getting bored with Ole Henry," Al told me. Vi is her mother. Her real name's Virginia.

7

Ole Henry has been taking Vi out for quite a while. He's in Sportswear. Al's mother is in Better Dresses.

"How come?" I said.

"Well, last night he stopped by right after we'd finished dinner. His timing was a little off, which, as you know"—she gave me her owl's eye—"doesn't happen very often. And my mother gave him a frankfurter and some sauerkraut, and I happen to know for a fact there was plenty of roast beef left over. You should've seen Ole Henry's bird-dog nose sniffing. He said, 'I thought I smelled roast beef,' and Vi looked straight at him and smiled and said, 'Must be the neighbor's.' So that ought to tell you something. I think the romance is over."

"Ole Henry is too old for your mother," I said. "She looks very young for her age."

"I'll tell her you said that. She already likes you, but that will definitely cement your friendship," Al said. She leaned past me. "Where's that dumb bus?" she said.

"She likes me?" I was pleased. "I didn't know that." Al's mother usually calls me "dear." When I first knew her, I thought it was because she didn't remember my name. But I guess she calls me "dear" because she likes me. That was nice of her.

"You're putting me on," I said. "Does she really like me?"

"She says you're a good solid kid who has her head on straight."

"That doesn't sound like your mother," I said.

"Actually"—Al looked over the top of her glasses at me—"she said she thought you were a very nice child with lovely manners. And you know my mother has a manners fetish."

"No kidding? She really said that? Remind me to tell my mother."

"She also said she liked having you drop in on her. She enjoys you, she said. But I told her she should see you when the moon is full." Al dipped her tongue down into the cone, then handed it to me for a dip.

"And when the tide is high. I mentioned the way your fangs start growing and horns sprout out of your head and you bay at the moon when you take a minute off from stirring the foul-smelling brew in your cauldron. You know what she said?"

I shook my head.

"She said she admired you very much."

I could feel myself blush. It's one thing to like someone. It's another thing entirely to admire someone.

"I don't believe you," I said. "Better polish off that cone. Don't forget what happened last time."

Al crossed her eyes. "Have I ever lied to you?" she said.

"No," I said, "but there's always a first time."

"Here comes our bus," Al said and shoved the cone into her mouth, chewing like mad.

chapter two.

The last time Al took an ice cream cone onto the bus, a man sitting in back of us gave her a hard time about eating on public transportation. He said it was against the law. So Al had flipped the cone back into her mouth the way a kid in our class did. Only in her case, she almost barfed all over her coat and it happened to be a brand-new coat that her mother had bought on sale. I can still remember how she looked, her eyes all bugged out and her face red.

But she made it. Good thing. I told her her mother would have killed her if she'd barfed on that coat.

"If my mother ever paid full price for anything," Al once told me, on account of her mother bought everything on sale, "I think she'd jump off the George Washington Bridge."

Sometimes Al exaggerates. Not always.

Al and I live in the same apartment building. She and her mother moved down the hall from us more than six months ago. We've been best friends ever since. I have a feeling we'll be friends all our lives, until we're old and rickety and have grandchildren. My mother has two friends she's known ever since she was younger than we are now. Al is a year older than me, but we're in the same grade, due to the fact that she moved a lot when she was little so she lost a grade somewhere along the line. I hope we stay friends forever.

The bus driver let us off and we started to walk.

We had almost reached our block when Al suddenly leaned over and spit something into her hand. It was the remains of the mocha chip cone.

"You didn't try that trick again!" I cried. "You're nuts."

Al looked at me sadly. "Someday I'll pull it off," she said. "Just for the record, that stunt isn't as easy as it looks. Life is full of things that aren't as easy as they look."

"Mr. Richards!" I shouted.

Al stumped glumly along. "That gives you another point," she said.

Every time we spot a Mr. Richards quote, we get a point. Mr. Richards was the assistant super in our

11

building when Al moved in. When he showed us how he polished the kitchen floor, he told us it wasn't as easy as it looked. He was right. When we tried to do it, we couldn't. Al and I and Mr. Richards were friends. Then he died. Things haven't been quite the same since.

We walked slowly.

"Maybe you'll get a letter today," I said.

Al pulled both her hands out of her pockets and held them up. The thumbs were tucked under. She'd read somewhere that if you make a wish when your thumbs are tucked under, the wish will come true.

"I doubt it," she said, but she smiled. I could tell she thought maybe today really was her lucky day and she *would* get a letter.

A couple of dudes wearing high-heeled shoes and black leather jackets were walking toward us.

"Hey hey, looka that!" they said. They didn't act as if they were really enthusiastic. They just said the words as if they'd rehearsed a lot. We looked behind us and across the street. A thin lady was walking her dog, and a big fat mother was pushing her baby. They must mean the hey hey for us. Pathetic.

Al flashed her bilious eye, but I guess it'd lost some of its power due to overuse because these dudes went on saying hey hey until we turned into our building.

chapter three.

It seems that ever since I've known Al, she's been waiting for a letter. First, it was her father she wanted so badly to hear from. Her mother and father are divorced. He was always on a trip somewhere and sent Al things: postcards and Mexican jumping beans and candy she wasn't supposed to eat. On account of she was a little on the plump side.

Then last month her father got married again, and he asked Al to the wedding. At first she said she might not go because her father had walked out on her and her mother when Al was little. Then she changed her mind and went. It was a good thing too. She made friends with Louise, the woman her father married, and also with Louise's three little boys, Nick, Chris, and Sam. Sam was Al's favorite. He was seven. When they took her to the airport to say good-bye, they all kissed her. Even Chris, and he's ten, and everybody knows ten-year-old boys don't go around kissing people indiscriminately. Look at my brother Teddy. He's almost ten. He practically only kisses my mother on Christmas and birthdays.

Then Louise and the boys had asked Al to come back in the summer for a visit. That was the second letter that didn't arrive. Louise said she'd put the invitation in writing. I've been telling Al that with all the work Louise has to do on the farm, with the cows and a pig and a barn and everything, she just hasn't gotten around to writing.

"She will," I told her about ten times. "You wait. One of these days you'll get a letter saying you're supposed to come and stay for a month or something."

Al also met a boy at the wedding. His name was Brian. He was fifteen. He mowed Louise's lawn. He had asked Al for her address so he could write to her. She said the reason he'd done that was that he'd had a glass of champagne. So had Al. It made her very talkative. She called me up from the wedding to give me the details, and I thought she'd never shut up.

Anyway, Al gave Brian her address written on a tiny piece of paper. So far, he hasn't written either. Every day she goes home from school and checks the

14

mail. The way she used to do when I first met her.

Al had showed me a bunch of pictures she'd taken of Louise and her father and the boys.

"They're a little out of focus," she said.

That, as my father would say, was a masterpiece of understatement. They looked as if they were swimming underwater.

"If you sort of close your eyes and hold this one sideways," Al said, handing me a picture, "you can make out my father. He has his arm around Louise."

I followed orders. Al's father and Louise looked like ghosts.

"This one," Al had said, her voice different, "is Brian."

I squinted and put the picture of Brian up to my face. Then I held it at arm's length. Brian looked like an astronaut about to put his big toe on the moon.

"He's much better looking than that," Al said.

"That's good," I said.

I wished Brian would write to Al. It would make my life easier. Every day no letter arrived. And every day I told her he probably had lost that tiny piece of paper with her address on it. So how could he write?

"He could get my address from my father," Al would say.

"He might not want to ask."

"If I wanted an easy out," Al would tell me, "I'd believe you. I want to but I don't. I guess I was just a one-night stand. Another pretty face." She'd scowl at me. I couldn't help laughing.

If people make promises to write, they should follow through. It's mean to do what they're doing to Al. She's counting on hearing from Louise and her father and Brian. Maybe Brian got cold feet. But that's no excuse for the others.

"Listen," I said to Al as we rode up in the elevator, "let me know if you get a letter, OK?"

As if she could keep it to herself for a second.

"You'll be able to hear me screaming," she said. "Everybody in the apartment will hear me. They'll probably send the super up to see what's wrong." She gave me the peace sign, and I went into my apartment.

"Better call Polly before she explodes," my mother said. "She's called twice. She sounds as if she's going to have a nervous breakdown if she doesn't speak to you. I asked if she wanted to leave a message, but she said no, she had to talk directly to you."

"Polly always sounds like that," I said. Polly Peterson is my second best friend next to Al. She lives on the West Side and is going to be a chef.

"You'll never guess!" Polly said, answering on the first ring. "My mother and father are going to Africa for six weeks." Polly's father is in the diplomatic service and whips around the world the way most people go to the supermarket.

"Do you get to go?" I asked. I'd be afraid to go to

Africa. I'm scared of lots of things. Airplanes and people I don't know and some big dogs. Not all. Just some. I'm trying to overcome my fears and not doing too well. Polly isn't scared of anything. That's one of the reasons I like her.

Polly sighed and the telephone vibrated.

"They say no. It's too expensive, for one thing. For another, they're going into some areas that might be dangerous. They're going on safari too. That's what I'd like. To see the lions and tigers up close."

I shivered. "Maybe you'd see a tribal war," I said.

"I doubt it," Polly said. "Anyway, when they decide they don't want me along, they make up excuses. The crux of the matter"—I could hear Polly breathing heavily, like an obscene phone caller—"the truth of it is that if I went, I'd miss the last few weeks of school and they're on a college kick."

"A college kick?" Polly and I and Al and practically everybody we know are in the seventh grade. With any luck at all, next year we'll be in the eighth. It was a little early to start worrying about college.

"My father says, 'Look at Evelyn. If we'd been stricter with Evelyn, she might've gone to college and not be going from pillar to post, unable to make up her mind where to light.'" Polly made slurping sounds. I could hear ice rattling around in a glass.

"What're you drinking?" I said.

"A little shooter of Coke," Polly said. "To get me through my homework. I get a sinking spell around this time of day, and a shooter of Coke helps."

"Mr. Richards," I said under my breath. That was another point for me. Mr. Richards always said "shooter of Coke."

"The thing of it is," Polly went on, "they took Evelyn everywhere with them when they traveled. I was left home with a nurse like some little wimp. But Evelyn hit every fleshpot in Europe, Asia, and Africa, not to mention North and South America. Look what good it did her," Polly said.

Evelyn is Polly's sister. She's so far out she's in. She has lived with a number of people. I mean boys. Polly's parents are liberal. Or Liberals. Whatever. Her mother just recently hyphenated her last name. She was going to resume her maiden name but figured after all these years of being Mrs. Peterson maybe nobody would know who she was when she said she was Ms. Hicks. So now she's known as Ms. Hicks-Peterson. She's going back to college in between trips to get her degree in sociology. She says her brain is tired and it may be some time before she gets it. But she's trying. That's what counts.

Polly says her father doesn't care what she calls herself as long as it doesn't cost him anything.

"Evelyn just bombed out of ballet school," Polly said. "Now she wants to be a photographer. You know Evelyn. She really gets into whatever occupation the person she's currently living with is involved in."

"When she lived with that guy in Boston," I reminded Polly, "Evelyn was studying ballet, and he wasn't a ballet dancer."

"Yeah," Polly said, "but he wore a leotard."

She sighed. "Anyway, they say no soap. I've got to stay here."

"Who're you staying with?" I asked.

There was a long pause. Polly is very direct. She says what she means. She never beats around the bush like some people I know. Al is like that too. No subterfuge, as my mother says. Everything is laid out, right in front of you. Polly never hints. I hate people who hint. Martha Moseley, a girl in my class, is a famous hinter.

"I want to stay with you," Polly blurted out. "Do you think it'd be OK? My mother would pay for the food and stuff. It'd only be for two weeks. Until school's over. Then I'm going up to the Cape to stay with my aunt and uncle. I could go to school easily. Just hop on the crosstown bus and presto, there I am. I promise I won't be any trouble. I won't leave my shoes under the table or anything."

Polly has been at my house often enough to know it drives my father bonkers to have people leave their shoes under the table. He says he belongs to the old school where people kept their shoes on until they went to bed at night. In some ways my father is very old-fashioned.

"What about Thelma?" I said. Thelma is Polly's

19

best friend now that she lives on the West Side, and Al is my best friend. Thelma is all right if you like the type. Thelma is very boy-crazy, I'm sorry to say. This only happened when she started to develop a chest.

"Thelma," Polly said. "Thelma is too big for her britches."

"That's probably because she buys them a size too small," I said.

Polly laughed. "That's a snide remark," she said. "I'm going to tell her you said that. She deserves to be taken down a peg. She's started to frizz her hair and wear eye shadow."

"Eye shadow? At her age? That's the weirdest thing I ever heard of." I shook my head. Lipstick I could believe. But eye shadow?

"She puts it on after she leaves home in the morning. That's the kind of girl she is. If you're going to wear it, load it on and face the music, I say. I don't know about Thelma," Polly said.

There was more here than met the eye. I'd get the details later, when Polly came to stay.

"I'll ask my mother," I said. "I'll soften her up, set the table, scrub the bathtub—all those little things that endear kids to their mothers. Then I'll slip it to her so smoothly she won't know what happened. Call you back."

"You are a true friend," Polly said with a catch in her voice. Polly is the least emotional person I know, but I think she would've started to cry if my mother

20

hadn't called me to say I better get off the phone, she was expecting a call. I think sometimes when she says that she's not telling the truth. It's just a suspicion I have. I would never accuse her of it.

"I'll call you tomorrow," I said.

"What's on Polly's mind?" my mother said when I'd hung up.

"Oh, her parents are going to Africa," I said.

"How exciting! I suppose she's going along. Those people lead exotic lives," my mother said. She and my father met Polly's parents once when we were going to the same school. My parents are conservative, and Polly's, as I said, are very liberal. Polly and I stood around the punchbowl at the parents' meeting and watched them eye each other. We were nervous as cats. I mean, they were all great people. But all they had in common was a couple of wimpy daughters. They talked and laughed, mostly about us, I guess. After we got home that night my mother's eyebrows zoomed up when I told her Polly's mother was against marriage. I thought they'd shoot right up underneath her hair and fly around the ceiling.

"If she's against marriage," my mother had said in her frostiest tone, "why'd she get married?" Then she ruffled up her hair in the back the way she does when she's agitated.

"Oh, not for herself," I said, sorry I'd opened my big mouth. "For Evelyn. Polly's sister. She lives with boys." Again my mother's eyebrows took flight.

"Evelyn went to Boston to study ballet, and Polly's mother said they never should have let her go because now she wants to marry the boy she's living with because people get married a lot in New England and Polly's mother doesn't think Evelyn's mature enough for a permanent relationship."

I knew I should shut up. I couldn't. Every word I said I could see was creating a bigger gulf between Polly's mother and mine. It didn't seem to matter much at the time. Now it did. It would be a lot easier to get my parents to say Polly could stay with us if my mother didn't have her back up about Polly's mother.

"I think I better go start my homework," I said. In all of my life I've never known my mother to argue against that. Before I started, I locked myself inside the bathroom. The bathroom, in my opinion, is the most restful room in the house. Nobody can get to you while you're inside. How do they know what you're doing? How do they know whether you're going to the bathroom or staring at yourself in the mirror, wondering what Mr. Richards saw in you that made him say you might be a model someday, or whether you're busy squeezing zits?

They don't. That's why it's restful.

"Telephone," my mother called. I opened the door as if she'd shouted, "Fire!"

"I didn't hear it ring," I said.

22

She smiled. "It didn't. I wanted to see how fast you'd move if I told you it had."

I was shocked.

"That's dishonest," I told her. "And you know it. If I did that to you, you'd give me a lecture."

But then the telephone really *did* ring.

"No letter today," Al said. "*Nada.* Not even an offer for a reduced rate for a *Playboy* subscription. Or even *House Beautiful*. A big fat zero. Are you doing anything?"

"I *was* in the bathroom," I said. "But my mother pulled a fast one. She told me somebody wanted me on the phone and it hadn't even rung."

"Your mother has unexpected depths," Al said in an admiring tone. "She has a streak of cunning I wouldn't have dreamed of."

"Yeah," I said.

"As mothers go," Al said, "yours is a nonconformist."

This is the highest praise Al can bestow. She sets great store on being a nonconformist, which is a person who doesn't follow the herd. When I first met her, she told me she was a nonconformist, the way other people would say they're a Democrat or a Republican.

"What's up?" I said.

"I want to come over," she said. "I have something to discuss."

I could tell from her voice that whatever it was she wanted to discuss was important.

"I want to read you a letter," she said.

"I thought you just said you didn't get a letter today," I said.

"I didn't. I said I wanted to come over and read you a letter. I didn't say I *got* a letter. I said I wanted to read one to you. That's not the same thing."

Al was being mysterious.

"Sure," I said. "Get over here on the double."

"What happened about the homework?" my mother asked.

"That can wait," I said. "It's Al. She needs advice. She's coming right over."

I could see from my mother's face she was going to give me an argument.

"Mom," I said, "what are friends for if you can't call on them in your hour of need?"

I knew that would get her and it did.

chapter four.

Almost before I had the words out of my mouth, Al rang her special ring: two, then one, then two. She's as speedy as a gazelle when the spirit moves her.

"Hi," she said to my mother, and we zapped silently into my room and closed the door.

I sat on the bed. Al paced. In a minute she'd have to go to the bathroom. When she's clutched, which she was now, she paces and then has to go to the bathroom. It never fails.

"Hey," I said, "I haven't got all day."

Al looked sheepish, which she did very well, due to the fact her bangs needed trimming. Her glasses were all steamed up. She thumped around the edges of the rug and stared at the ceiling. This is an old trick of hers. You'd almost think there were words written up there, the way she acts.

Her eyes, behind the steamy glasses, were enormous.

"I wrote to him," she said. "Just in case. You know. To have it ready to mail in case he writes to me." She gazed off into the distance.

Then, all of a sudden, she snapped, "Who says the boy has to write first?"

"Nobody," I said.

"What's all this equality business if a girl can't write first if she happens to feel like it? What's the ERA all about anyway if I can't write a letter to a kid if I want to? It's all a sham, a pile of baloney, if you ask me."

"You're right," I said. "Absolutely right."

It's tough to argue if everybody agrees with everybody else. Al sat down beside me. "I might not feel like mailing it. But if I do, I've got it ready in case the spirit moves me. Right?"

"Sure," I said.

"Of course, there's always the chance he might write me first. I doubt it but there's always the chance. He probably won't. But still."

I've done that. When I want something to happen very much, I tell myself it won't. That way I prepare myself for disappointment. It doesn't work very well, but I do it anyway.

"I want to read it to you to see what you think. I'll be back in a sec." She zapped down the hall to the bathroom. When she got back, she unfolded a piece of yellow lined paper that looked as if it'd been buried in the backyard during the Civil War.

"Listen to this," she said. "Are you listening?"

I nodded.

" 'Brian, old buddy,' " Al said, giving me a piercer. "What do you think of that for starters?"

It was a tense moment. I had to watch my step.

"Well," I said slowly, "the only trouble with that is he might think it was a letter from his old camp counselor or somebody like that. Why don't you just say 'Dear Brian'?"

"Because that might give him the wrong idea." She sat down beside me. "Now just listen and don't interrupt, all right?"

" 'Brian, old buddy, you probably don't remember me.' " She stopped and gave me another piercer, waiting for me to say something.

I looked at my fingernails and thought of emptying my wastebasket, which could've used it, and decided no.

"How's that?" she demanded.

I chose my words carefully.

"I think it's too mushy," I said.

"Listen." She pinched my arm. "Just listen. 'You probably don't remember me. I met you at my father's wedding. I had to take off my shoes because they were killing my feet. They were red.' "

"What were, the shoes or the feet?" I said.

"Hush," Al said, glaring.

" 'I had on a red-and-white checked dress and am sort of plump,' " she continued.

I'm no expert but I thought her letter was a bummer. I may be a year younger than Al, but, personally, I could've written a better letter myself—with both hands tied behind me. And, believe me, I haven't had any more practice writing letters to boys than she has. I didn't want to put the kibosh on her letter entirely, but I figured, as her best friend, it was up to me to tell her tactfully.

"That's to refresh his memory," she said. "What do you think?"

"Why don't you tell him you wear glasses and have a nose like a wombat?" I said. "That'd make him sit up and take notice."

"I never should've asked you," Al said in a huff. "I should've known better. I didn't ask for any sarcastic comments. I asked for your honest opinion."

I threw tact to the winds.

"I think it stinks," I said.

"You haven't heard it all," she said. "Don't make up your mind until you've heard it all."

"OK. Go on. I promise I won't say anything until you're finished."

Al wriggled her bottom around, making a little nest for herself. "This is the last part. I'm not too sure

28

about it. It could be a stroke of genius. On the other hand, it could be the kiss of death. See what you think."

She cleared her throat.

" 'In case you feel like answering' "—she gave me a significant look over the top of her glasses—" 'I enclose a self-addressed envelope. Please excuse no stamp.' "

The room was filled with silence. I could feel her looking at me. Finally I said, "I guess that's a smart move. What with the postal rates going up and everything."

She nodded. "Are you ready for the coup de grace? You want to hear how I signed it?"

I nodded back.

"Now hear this." She spoke slowly, enunciating every word. "I signed it 'Your pal, Al.' That's so he'll know this is going to be a platonic friendship."

She gripped my arm and dug in her fingers. "Also, that tells him I don't care whether he answers my letter or not. Don't you think that's good? It sounds nice and casual. 'Your pal, Al.' I like that."

"Why don't you sign it 'Your old pal, Al'?" I suggested. "That sounds even more as if you don't care whether he answers or not. It goes with the beginning, too. You know. Old buddy, old pal. How platonic can you get?" I used my most sarcastic voice, but Al was so wrapped up in her letter nothing seemed to get through to her.

"Excellent," Al said, beaming. "Excellent. What would I do without you? You're a genius." She scratched at the paper, erasing so hard she poked a big hole through it.

She wrote in "Your old pal, Al."

"I've got to get home right away and type this up. There's not a moment to lose."

I couldn't believe she was really going to send the letter. It was so bad. If she mailed it, maybe Brian would be so embarrassed he'd throw it in the trash, or maybe, if he was a rotten type, he'd take it to school and show it to his friends and they'd laugh. At Al. I couldn't bear the thought. On the other hand, maybe he would be pleased to get a letter from a girl he barely knew. You had to look at all sides of a problem like this.

Al was out the door and through the living room so fast I didn't have a chance to tell her about Polly. On her way she almost knocked Teddy down. He was sniveling around, as usual, because the cookie jar was empty. This always upsets him.

"Holy Toledo!" Teddy shouted, bobbing and weaving. "Who the Sam Hill was that?"

In addition to many of his other undesirable traits, Teddy is also a copycat. He picks up all his expressions from Al and me. I doubt seriously if he's ever thought up anything original. If he weren't my blood brother, I probably wouldn't even speak to him. He's the wimp of the Western world, in my opinion. My mother says I should be patient with him, that I was once nine myself. I know this to be true. But I find it difficult to believe I was ever as repulsive as he is.

"That was a burglar," I told him. "I caught him going through my jewelry box and scared him off."

"It was?" Teddy's forehead was corrugated, due to the fact he was thinking. It takes a lot out of Teddy when he's forced to think. You can practically see the lines forming on his little face, aging him before his time.

See what I mean? It's a very humbling thing, having Teddy for a brother.

chapter five.

"Mom," I said, "I'm finished with the carrots. What do you want me to do now?" I was killing my mother with kindness, working her around the head and shoulders with TLC, softening her up for the big Polly push. "How about if I iron some napkins?" I like to iron napkins and actually am very good at it. Most people think you're crazy if you say you like to iron napkins. There's something about lining up the edges so all the corners match that interests me. Soothes me, even. That, plus the smell. The smell of ironing is the best part. When I was younger and much more naïve, my mother used to pay me five cents an hour to iron napkins. Now she expects it as her due.

My mother looked at me suspiciously.

"What do you want from me?" she said.

"Nothing. I just feel like doing things. You're a good woman, Ma," I told her. She likes to be told that. Besides, it's true.

"How about cleaning out the fridge?" she said.

I opened the door and sniffed. "Nothing smells," I said. In our house we have a rule. Never clean out the fridge until something smells high as a kite.

"I told you about Polly's parents going to Africa, didn't I?" I said casually.

"Aha. Now we're getting down to the nitty-gritty. You want to go with them. Is that it?"

"Are you kidding? They didn't even ask me. I wouldn't go to Africa on a bet," I said. "I'd be scared. Besides, you know Dad. He'd say we couldn't afford it. If I asked for money to go to Brooklyn, he'd say we couldn't afford it. Much less Africa."

She laughed. "You're right," she said.

"I was wondering—" I began.

"Yes," she said, giving me her undivided attention. "Go on."

"I was just wondering," I began again, "if, when her parents go away, if Polly could stay with us. It'd only be for two weeks," I said hastily, seeing from her face she was thinking of all kinds of reasons why

Polly shouldn't stay with us. "She could take the crosstown bus to school. Then when school's out, she's going up to the Cape to stay with her aunt and uncle. Oh, please, Mom! Please!" I hugged her until she cried. "Stop, you're hurting!" I used to hug her a lot when I was little. Lately I haven't been doing it as much.

"I don't know," my mother said when I let her go. "That's a tremendous responsibility, taking on someone else's child in this day and age. Think of all the things that could go wrong."

"What?" I said. "Polly's had her appendix out and everything."

"Besides, I don't even know her mother and father."

"You've met them," I reminded her. "Anyway, I don't want Polly's mother and father to stay with us. It's Polly I want. They're nice people. Very nice. And very strict," I said, not entirely truthfully. I've noticed my mother and father lean toward parents who are strict.

"They have different ideas, different standards, different rules for Polly," my mother said, pursing her mouth. "Polly has led a very sophisticated life."

"I don't see what difference that makes. Polly is the salt of the earth," I said. "You like her. You said you did. Plus she's a terrific cook." I could tell from my mother's face I'd hit home.

"While she's here—that is, if you decide to let

her—you can give a dinner party. Polly will be the chef. I'll wait on table. You won't have to do a thing except dress up and smile a lot and accept compliments on the cuisine. How would that be?"

I could see she was tempted. My mother gets uptight when she has friends in for dinner. My father, Teddy, and I stay out of her way as much as possible. She usually tries a brand-new dish, something exotic and complicated that requires a lot of chopping and grating and mincing and that throws her into a tizzy. We tell her she should give the guests meat loaf or stuffed cabbage or one of the old faithfuls. But she gives us the hairy eyeball and goes right on chopping, grating, and mincing, her lips tight, her sense of humor gone.

"How would that be?" I asked her, squeezing her harder. I might squeeze out a yes if I tried hard enough.

"I'll talk to your father," she said.

"Mom, you know Dad. If he thinks it's all right with you, it'll be OK with him. You're the one who can bring him around and you know it. Besides," I said, "he likes Polly. He even said he missed her being around so often. She said she promised if you let her stay she won't take off her shoes and leave them lying around."

"We'll see," she said.

That night we had corned beef and cabbage. My father's favorite. Music hath charms to soothe the savage beast, they say. Food also hath likewise charms.

"There's no place in town where the groceries are any better than right here," my father said. My mother smiled. It's always nice to be appreciated, I guess.

After dinner I cleared the table while Teddy crumbed. Teddy is a crummy crumber. When he finishes wiping off the crumbs, the rug looks as if we'd just had a blizzard.

Teddy is also teaching himself to whistle. He whistled off-key the entire time he was crumbing. It's very hard for me to imagine Teddy grown up. Just think. Someday this little monster might even be a father. Another little Teddy will be foisted on an unsuspecting world. It's enough to give a person palpitations.

"Did you ask him yet?" I hissed as my mother came into the kitchen for coffee.

"Ask him what?" Teddy said at the top of his lungs. He says most things that way.

"Calm down," my mother said and went back to the living room. I could hear them talking. It would be neat to have Polly stay for two weeks. We could put up a cot in my room and talk for hours in the dark. It would be like being in boarding school. I've read a lot of books about kids in boarding school. They were always getting brownies from home and having crushes on teachers and playing field hockey.

36

It sounded cool. Then we could put another cot in my room and Al could sleep over and it'd be like being in a dormitory. We could eat snacks under the covers and talk about a whole bunch of things we don't want our parents to know we know about. It'd be a blast.

My father came into the kitchen to get more coffee.

"What's this I hear about the pride of West End Avenue coming to bunk in with you?" he said. That's what he's called Polly ever since she moved to the West Side.

Did that mean it was settled?

"Isn't that great, Dad?" I said.

"I'm not sure. Two of you in one room sounds like a lot of distraction to me. And what you don't need, my pet, is any more distraction than you already have."

"Polly's a very good student," I said, casting down my eyes demurely. Parents always like it if your friends are good students. They think some of it might rub off on you. Usually they're wrong. "And her mother and father are very anxious for her to keep up her marks so she can get into a good college." Sometimes I amaze myself at how phony I can be.

I clasped my hands in front of me, as if I were preparing to read aloud some crummy poem I'd made up.

"Her parents are very strict, like you and Mom," I

37

went on. "They don't stand for any nonsense."

My father grunted.

"I seem to remember you telling us about what a kook Polly's sister is," he said, dredging the depths of his memory and coming up with a goody. Most times he acts as if he's dressed in a space suit equipped with earplugs. Then bang! Total recall. You can't count on him.

I took the line of least resistance and didn't answer. I kept smiling, though. When in doubt, keep smiling. I'm planning on having this slogan, which is my own invention, made up into a bumper sticker. When you think about it, it's really quite profound.

My father took his coffee back into the living room.

"Polly is one of my favorite children," I could hear my mother say. Then my father said something I couldn't catch.

"Of course, Africa is a long way away. If any emergency arose. You're right."

My mother lowered her voice. How about that? They didn't even trust me. They thought I was eavesdropping.

Silence.

"It's up to you," my father said. "You're the one who gets the burden of having another person to look out for. If it doesn't bother you, well, I guess it's all right with me."

I couldn't resist. I strolled into the living room. "Anything I can get for you?" I asked.

"I'll tell you one thing," my father said, pointing at me. "If your friend Polly comes, there has to be complete understanding that what we say goes. Whether she likes it or not, Polly will have to toe the line and obey our rules."

"She won't even take off her shoes and leave them under the table," I said. "She promised."

My father looked surprised.

"Sounds as if you already have things arranged," he said.

"Oh, Dad!" I threw my arms around my father and kissed him.

"Here, here. What makes me so loved and wanted all of a sudden?" he said.

"How come she gets a friend to sleep over?" Teddy whined. "Why can't I?"

He gathered his face together to make a scene.

"Ted," I whispered. "If you'll be a good boy, I'll give you something." For his age, Teddy is extremely materialistic.

He ran his arm underneath his nose in lieu of a handkerchief. I closed my eyes. Too much.

"What?" he said.

I was dialing Polly's number. The phone rang and rang. They must be out.

I was about to hang up when Polly answered.

"The answer is yes. Yes you may stay with us for two weeks if you'll be good and not divert me from my studies and not eat too much and help with the housework and a few other things," I said.

"Keen!" Polly cried. "Oh, I'm so glad! Now all I have to do is get the OK from my mother. I think she's planning to ask my old nanny to sit with me."

"Nanny?" I said. "Is that what you call your grandmother?"

"No, it's what I call my nurse," Polly said.

"I didn't know you'd been sick."

"I haven't been, turd," Polly said. "I had a nurse when I was little. We called her nanny because when she came to work for us we were living in England where people have nannies, and now she lives here except she's so old she's practically ancient. Tell your mother I'll make her favorite dinner and wash the dishes and take care of Teddy and everything."

"I already have," I said. "Poll, there's one thing I want to know, though."

"Anything. Ask me anything," Polly said.

"Do you do windows?" I said.

chapter six.

"I made a carbon copy," Al told me next morning on our way to school. "I make carbons of all my letters and keep them on file. Just in case I write a book. Or somebody tries to sue me for breach of promise. You never know when one of those copies might come in handy."

"Are you going to mail it?" I asked.

"I haven't made up my mind. Maybe I will. Maybe not. Anyway, I want to read it over a couple of times, make sure I've got it right. A letter is a very tricky thing. It can create good will, and a bad letter can also ruin a friendship. Never underestimate the power of the apt word, baby."

That's the difference between me and Al. When I write a letter, which isn't often, I just sit down and write it and mail it off. Al studies all the angles. She makes letter writing sound like a United Nations project.

"If I mailed it today," Al said, "it'd get there the day after tomorrow. On the other hand, if I mail it tomorrow, the weekend will come in between so it wouldn't get there until Monday. Or maybe even Tuesday."

"Suppose it gets lost?" I said. "My aunt in Colorado wrote a letter to my mother and it never arrived. It was just swallowed up along the way. Did you think of that?"

"You're some help," Al said. "If I do mail it today or tomorrow, I can expect a reply not later than the following Tuesday, or Wednesday, at the latest. Or possibly Thursday, at the outside."

Oh, boy. Next week would be tense.

"Maybe he won't be able to answer right away," I said. "Maybe he has lots of lawns to mow or tests to study for. You can't tell."

"Or maybe," Al said in her dark voice, "he might be busy making goo-goo eyes at some girl."

"Is he the goo-goo-eye type?"

"No, he's shy," Al said proudly, as if she were saying, "He's brilliant," or "He's handsome."

"He's the kind that girls throw themselves at, though," she added.

"How do you know?"

"He's aloof," she said, as if that explained everything. "Aloof boys always have girls throwing themselves at them. It's a law of nature. Didn't you know that?"

How could I know that when I wasn't even sure what "aloof" meant?

It was a beautiful morning, soft and clear, smelling nice. I could see a jet's vapor trail starting high up, coasting slowly toward the horizon.

"How about if we play hooky?" I said. "I can't stand the thought of going to school."

Al stopped walking.

"What'll we do if we do?" she asked.

"We could go to Radio City Music Hall and see the Rockettes," I said, after some thought.

"The trouble with the Rockettes," Al said, "is they're conformists. Every last one. They have to be, to be hired. You get a Rockette who doesn't feel like kicking with her left leg just because all the rest of 'em are and you've got a big problem. She louses up the whole line. Think about it."

How did we get started on this? I wondered.

"Just imagine what would happen if once, only once, you get this nonconforming Rockette who wants to liven things up a bit. So she kicks with her left when the rest of the girls are kicking with their right and first thing you know, her leg gets tangled with the leg next to her and the whole line topples.

Goes crashing down right there on the stage. Boy, that'd make the evening news!"

"I get the mental picture," I said. "Scratch Radio City. I can't afford it, plus I didn't know I was going to have to listen to an anti-Rockette lecture, for Pete's sake." We continued our creep toward school.

"Watch the dog-do," I warned Al. She was thrashing around inside her book bag and didn't hear me. She stepped splat into a gigantic dog turd.

"Disgusting," she said. "People have no business having a dog in the city, even if they're supposed to pick up after them. They should be walking down dirt roads, running through green fields, barking at cows, stuff like that."

"Sounds like a dog's life to me," I said.

"Wait'll Mr. Keogh gets a whiff of me," Al said, scraping her shoe on the curb. "He'll throw me out of class."

"We can wipe off your shoe when we get to the girls' room," I told her. "Listen, I forgot to tell you my news yesterday, you left in such a hurry. Guess who's coming to stay with us for two weeks."

"Robert Redford," Al guessed.

"No, silly. Someone you like. Take a guess."

"I like Robert Redford. He's a little on the short side, I understand, but he's cute."

"I thought he was tall," I said. "He looks tall to me." I don't like being told things like Robert Redford's on the short side. I don't know why, but I don't.

"Nope," Al said. "He's about as tall as me."

I didn't believe her but I didn't want to get her sidetracked again.

"Take a guess," I said. "A real one."

"Dracula." Al bent down and wiped her shoe on a tiny piece of grass.

"No, drip." I couldn't hold out any longer. "Polly."

"Polly?" Al was suddenly still. Her hair hung over her face. "For two weeks? How come?"

"Well, Polly's mother and father are going to Africa, and they don't want her to come because it's so close to the end of school and she says they're on a college kick, due to her sister Evelyn being a floater and a drifter. Then she'll go up to the Cape to visit her aunt and uncle after school's over."

"Where's she going to sleep?"

"In my room, of course. We're going to put up a cot and we can all . . ."

Al took a long time wiping off her shoe. She kept her head down and scraped carefully.

"Well, I guess that means I won't be seeing much of you for a while," she said. "With Polly there and all."

"Don't be silly," I said. "It won't make any difference."

"That's what you think," she said. "Two's company, three's a crowd, don't forget."

"Polly's not like that," I said.

"You wait." She inspected her shoe. "It's going to be awful crowded," she said. "In your room. That's a teeny room."

"It's not so teeny," I said. "You've spent the night there plenty of times. It's not that teeny. You make it sound about the size of a jail cell."

"I never stayed there more than one night at a time," Al said. She still didn't look at me. "Personally, if it were me, I'd hate sharing my room for that long. You won't have any privacy."

"Who needs privacy? Polly's my friend. If I had a sister," I said, "I'd have to share my room with her. So what's the difference?"

"Polly is scarcely your sister," Al said in a cold voice I'd never heard her use before. Not even when she was mad at me. "Anyway, a sister's different. A sister you can't help. Anyone who has a sister will tell you that sisters fight a lot. Because they're together so much, probably. They have to share a closet and a bathroom and a bedroom and they get on each other's nerves. You and Polly, I expect, will fight a lot."

"I doubt it," I said. "What's the matter with you, anyway? I thought you'd be glad to hear that Polly was coming. I thought you liked her. You always did before. What made you so sour all of a sudden?"

Al took the steps two at a time. Her legs are longer than mine. I couldn't keep up.

46

When she got to the top, she turned.

"Just remember," she said. "Two weeks can be an awful long time. Two weeks can be an eternity."

"I thought you liked Polly," I said. "I thought she was your friend too. I was planning we'd all hang out together on the weekend and pretend we were in boarding school and sleeping in a dormitory and everything. It'd be fun."

Before Al had a chance to answer, a bunch of girls came toward us. It was Martha Moseley and some of her vassals.

"My cousin's having a Sweet Sixteen party," Martha said in her anchor person's voice. She looked at us, then turned away. "They're going to have it in a disco."

The vassals rolled their eyes at the wonder of it all. They sighed in unison.

"The club," Martha announced, "is going to be decorated like a disco. Posters, strobe lights, the works."

There was a hush while they digested that. Linda Benton crossed her hands on her chest and looked like Joan of Arc about to go into battle. Without her suit of mail. Sally Sykes shrieked, as if somebody had just pinched her on her bottom.

I looked at Al. Her face wore a closed expression, as if she were a thousand miles away.

"My cousin's mother bought her this gorgeous evening gown," Martha said. There was a long pause.

"It's strapless."

Again a great sigh. They were almost swooning.

Martha turned slowly, as if she were modeling her cousin's strapless evening gown.

"The invitations are going to read 'dressy attire,' " she said in what was for her a soft voice.

"OOOOOHHHHHH!"

Al stepped in as if the line had been written for her.

"What does that mean?" she snapped. "No bare feet?"

She turned her back on all of us and stomped inside.

When I caught up with her, she was thrashing around her locker, making a lot of noise and breathing heavily.

"The expression on Martha's face was a beaut," I told her. "You should've stuck around to see."

Al didn't answer. I put a finger in the middle of her back, very lightly. That drives her crazy.

"Cut it out!" she hollered, knocking my hand away. "Just you cut it out!"

"What's bugging you?" I said. When Al gets like that, I can't figure her out.

She picked up her books and started toward our home room. By the time I got myself organized with my sneakers and other gear, she had disappeared.

The hall was deserted.

The heck with her.

chapter seven.

I had soccer practice after school. Usually Al waits for me. This time she didn't. She doesn't take soccer. I made two goals.

"Keep it up," the coach said, "and you may make the first team."

All the way home I practiced soccer plays in my head. By the time I got to our building, I could see the headlines:

GIRL MAKES WORLD CUP TEAM. FIRST TIME EVER!

My mother was on the floor, doing her exercises. When I opened the refrigerator door, she shouted, "Don't touch the chicken salad! It's for dinner."

As if I would. I took my hand away from the chicken salad. "There's not too much there," I said.

My mother thumped her hips on the floor, which she says is very beneficial and keeps them in trim. The people in the apartment below us must be having fits.

"We're going out for dinner with the Hicks-Petersons," she said. "They're taking us to the snazziest restaurant in town."

"Who are they?"

"Polly's mother and father." She started on her sit-ups. "I called to extend the invitation to Polly, and her mother wasn't in so I left a message. When she called back, she said, 'This is Mary Hicks-Peterson,' and I drew a blank. Why didn't you tell me she was calling herself that?"

"What's the matter with your face?" I asked, not answering her question. "You look terrible."

"It's a facial. Draws out impurities. Erases lines."

"You're going to be the life of the party with that stuff on," I said. "Wait'll Dad gets a load of you. I hope the restaurant is dark. He might be embarrassed to be seen with you."

She finished her sit-ups. My mother doesn't take her exercises lightly. When she's through, she looks as if she'd just climbed Mount Kilimanjaro.

"Nineteen, twenty," she wheezed. "You know I can't talk and do sit-ups at the same time. I wash it off before I go," she said.

50

"Whew!" I said. "That's a relief."

She went into the bathroom to wash off her facial. I followed her.

"What did Polly's mother say?" I asked.

"She said, 'Will you and your husband be our guests tonight at dinner? Polly has told us of your invitation to house her while we're out of the country. My husband and I were planning to ask Nanny in to look after her, but she's so anxious to accept your lovely offer. It's really too good of you,'" my mother recited as if she'd learned the lines by heart.

"What did you say?" I asked, sitting on the edge of the bathtub.

"I said I thought it was really too good of us, too," she said.

"Mother! You didn't!"

"I can't see any change at all." She stared at herself in the mirror. "I look exactly the same. Maybe a little older."

"You look great," I told her. "What did you really say?"

"I said we would be pleased to have Polly stay as long as she understood the house rules. And Mrs. Hicks-Peterson said Polly was always talking about us, how much she liked us all, what a darling Teddy was—"

"Mother! I don't believe you. She never said that. Nobody in their right mind ever said that about Teddy and you know it."

"That's all you know. Now leave me while I compose myself and decide what I shall wear." My mother was pleased the Hicks-Petersons had asked her and Dad for dinner. So was I.

"You look smashing," my father told her as they got ready to leave. She did too.

"If you feel like splitting the chicken salad three ways," she said after reciting a long list of instructions, as I was in charge, "why don't you ask Al over for supper?"

"Maybe," I said. "I'll see."

"Why does she always have to come?" Teddy whined. "That means we have to split the Sara Lee cake three ways. I don't see why Al always has to come over and eat with us."

I hadn't been planning to invite Al for supper, but after listening to Teddy moan and groan, I decided I would.

Just to show him.

I zapped down the hall and rang her bell. After a couple of minutes Al's mother peeked through the peephole.

"Oh, it's you, dear," she said, opening up. "How nice to see you. How are you?"

She really did like me. Now that I knew she did, I could tell. Sometimes these things have to be pointed out. When you know someone likes you, it's awfully easy to like them back. I could tell from her face and the tone in her voice that she liked me.

She rested her hand on my arm.

"You smell good," I told her.

"I've just taken a tub," she said, smiling at me. That meant she had put a lot of bath oil and gunk in the water. To keep from drying up, I guess. Al's mother is very chic, being in Better Dresses, and has to think a lot about things like staying moist.

"Alexandra isn't home," she said. "She called to say she was staying at Nancy Bishop's for supper. She'll be home early, though, if you want to come back later."

Nancy Bishop is a super conformist. If she had the legs for it, she could easily be a Rockette. What was Al doing over there?

"That's OK," I said. "It wasn't anything important." And I went back to Teddy, the chicken salad, and the Sara Lee cake, which there was plenty of, after all.

chapter eight.

"Read me the one about the little kid who sells matches in the snow in her bare feet," Teddy pestered me. "Read that one. It's so sad," he said gleefully.

I wasn't going to. I've read it to him about a thousand times. He can read perfectly well if he wants to. He's lazy. Then God laid a hand on my head and made me sweet and gentle and sisterly. So I did.

Boy. Talk about violence and cruelty and all those things they feed kids today on the tube and elsewhere. All I can say is, whoever wrote this book of fairy tales was ahead of his time. He really knew how to sock it to the little ones. He would've had some residuals is all I know.

By the time I finished, Teddy's eyes were at half-mast. The minute I turned my back, I knew he'd be sucking his thumb.

I switched off the light and left his door open a crack. Teddy's thumb made slurpy noises against the roof of his mouth. He pretends he doesn't suck his thumb, but he does.

In a flash I flicked on the light.

"Caught you!" I said.

Teddy was down for the count. He didn't even have the strength to whine. I went into the living room and turned on the TV to help me stay awake until my mother and father got home.

"How was it?" I asked when they finally arrived.

My mother took off her shoes with a huge sigh of relief. She wears very high heels when she gets dressed up. They kill her feet but they flatter her legs, she says.

"Vanity, thy name is woman," my father says.

"Marvelous," she said, rubbing her toes. "Absolutely marvelous. I could've fed my entire family for a month on what that dinner cost, but it was worth it."

"Especially when Old Man Hicks-Peterson was footing the bill," said my father.

"Is it all set?" I asked. "When is Polly coming?"

"I had the vol-au-vent of sweetbreads, and, for dessert," my mother went on, "coupe Alexandra."

"That's nice," I said. "I'll tell Al there's a dessert named for her. When's Polly coming?"

"I wish I could afford wine like that," my father said.

I could see I wasn't getting through. They were like Cinderella coming home from the ball. I kissed them both good night and went to bed. I had a very realistic dream, which I sometimes do. In my dream Martha Moseley was wearing a strapless dress and dancing with Mr. Richards. She was taller than he was. It was fantastic. They were dancing an old-fashioned waltz or something that looked like a waltz. All of a sudden Mr. Richards let go of Martha and began to skate, as if he were polishing the kitchen floor. He'd tied rags around his shoes and he put his arms behind himself as if he were Hans Brinker and the Silver Skates. He went around and around, and Martha stood there with her mouth hanging open, just the way Teddy does.

"Take off that dress at once!" a girl shouted. It was Martha's cousin, who appeared from nowhere and began to tug at the dress.

"If you don't take off that dress, which is strapless," Al said, "you will definitely never get a letter from a boy. I am an expert on letters from boys and how they should be written. Make sure they understand you are a platonic friend. Always sign your letters 'Your old pal, Al,' " she said firmly.

"But my name's not Al," Martha said. For the first and last time in my life I felt kind of sorry for her.

"That's neither here nor there," Al said. She was in command of the situation. Mr. Richards skated close to them. "Have a weird day," Al said, and she and Mr. Richards skated out of sight. Martha stood there in her underwear and cried.

I woke up smiling. It was the best dream I've ever had. I wrote down what I could remember to tell Al. Sometimes, if you don't write down dreams immediately, they fade. I didn't want this one to fade. It was so real.

My mother had come down to earth by the time she hit the breakfast table. "Polly will be here on Friday," she said. "Her mother and father are taking off at midnight Friday. They're very nice people. Not at all uppity."

"Why'd you think they'd be uppity?" I said. "Polly's not uppity and she's their kid."

"Oh, I don't know." My mother can be very vague when it suits her. "They've traveled so much. Being in the diplomatic service must be fascinating. One expects they might be hoity-toity. But they're lovely. Very down-to-earth."

Whatever that means. You never know. One never knows.

I was a little surprised to see Al waiting for me. After yesterday I wasn't sure she would be. Also, she was wearing her yellow dress. Yellow is a happy color.

"You look nice," I told her as we set out.

"I had a dream about Mr. Richards last night," she said.

"I can't believe you did," I said. "So did I."

"You tell me your dream, I'll tell you mine," Al said. I told her about Martha Moseley dancing with Mr. Richards in her cousin's strapless dress.

"Then you stuck in your two cents," I said, "and told Martha when she wrote a letter to a boy, she should sign it 'Your old pal, Al,' and she said her name wasn't Al, and you said, 'That's neither here nor there.' "

We started to laugh, and we laughed so hard we almost cried. It was like the old days with Mr. Richards. He told us a good laugh is good for the soul. I believe it. People turned to stare.

When we'd calmed down and stopped for a red light to change, Al said, "Now it's my turn. Mr. Richards asked me if I wanted a shooter of Coke and a carrot stick. I said yes, that would be nice. Then he said to me, out of a clear sky, 'Them little fellas, them three little fellas, they dropped into your lap like a bunch of ripe pears.' That's what he said. 'Them little boys are like a gift from Heaven, as I see it. Not too many folks I know are as lucky as you are. Do you know that?' "

Al's eyes were wide and glittering. "It was like he was in the room with me." She turned to me. "How do you suppose he knew? About the boys, I mean."

I shook my head. "I don't know," I said. "I guess he just did."

"When I woke up," Al said, "I felt about a hundred per cent better than I did when I went to sleep."

I nodded. "I know," I said. "Me too. Isn't it strange we both dreamed about him the same night?"

"Absolutely bizarre," Al agreed. We crossed the street. "The funny thing is," she continued, "that for a long time I couldn't remember how his voice sounded. Right after he died I got it just right in my head. But in a while I couldn't hear his voice. I tried. I listened very hard. Nothing worked. But now I can hear him. Clear as a bell. It's the strangest thing."

I knew what she meant. It was the same with me.

"When's Polly coming over?" Al asked casually.

"Friday, after school," I answered just as casually. "How about coming over for supper so we can make plans?"

Al looked crestfallen.

"Nancy Bishop asked me to sleep over Friday," she said.

"Did you say you would?"

"Yeah," Al said glumly. "You know what she wants to be when she grows up?"

"A lion tamer?" I said, joking.

"A Rockette," Al said.

"That'd be good," I said. "She'd probably be a good one."

"Yeah," Al said. "She probably would."

chapter nine.

"Polly has her own TV set," I said at breakfast Friday morning. "In her bedroom."

"Eat your cereal, Teddy," my mother said.

I watched Teddy eat.

"Do you think he could stay with a friend?" I said. "While Polly's here, I mean. Not forever," I added, getting a look at my mother's face.

My father was reading the newspaper. He didn't say anything. In the morning he's usually silent.

"Do you think we could move our TV set into my bedroom? Just for a little bit?" I asked.

My mother made a face at me and shook her head.

My father kept on reading.

"My friend Hubie has bunk beds," Teddy said. His cowlick stood straight up like an antenna. "He sleeps in the top one. Only when he's alone, that is. When somebody sleeps over, he sleeps in the bottom one. Once he fell out. All he got was a bump on the head."

"He fell out of the top bunk and all he got was a bump on his head?" I said.

"No, he fell out of the bottom bunk and got a bump on his head," Teddy told me. "You don't listen."

He pushed back his chair. "I think I'll call Hubie up and ask him if I can sleep over in his top bunk."

"Stay where you are," my father said, not lifting his head.

"The only trouble with Hubie," Teddy said, staying where he was, "is that his mother doesn't believe in meat."

"Is that so?" my mother said. "Use your napkin."

"That's so," Teddy agreed. "She believes in fish and junk but she doesn't believe in meat. She says it clogs the arteries. She says you live longer if you don't eat meat. Hubie says he's going to live longer'n me. Once he went to McDonald's and ate two hamburgers and some French fries and right after he threw up. He started bawling because he thought he was going to die. Right there in McDonald's he thought he was going to die," Teddy said, his voice scornful. "I never heard of such a dumb thing."

He put his chin in his hand.

"It turned out Hubie was coming down with a virus," he said. "But his mother still doesn't believe in meat."

I took out the dirty dishes. Then I came back and sat down.

"You can rent a TV set by the week for not very much money," I said. "Al's mother was telling me about a friend of hers who had an operation and she rented a TV set for not very much at all."

My father finished his egg.

"We have one TV set and that's for the entire family," he said, looking at me.

"Polly's family has three," I said.

He got up from the table and came around to kiss my mother good-bye.

"Let's get one thing straight," he said. "We're us and Polly's family are them. We're not changing our life-style because she's coming to stay. And you're off to a bad start if you're going to compare our possessions and the way we do things. If I'd known this was going to happen, I would've put my foot down and said Polly couldn't come. Right from the beginning I would've said no. Don't make me sorry I said yes. Don't make me sorry before she even arrives. I may be late tonight," he said. "Just keep something hot."

After he'd gone, my mother said, "You should've known better."

"All I asked was if we could put the TV in my room

for a while," I said. "I didn't know he was going to make a federal case out of a simple request."

"That wasn't a simple request," she said, "and you know it."

"I think I should have my own TV set," Teddy said. "At the end of my bed so's I can wake up and watch cartoons early in the morning and not disturb anyone. So's I can stay warm and cozy in my bed and not have to get up and go all the way out to the living room to watch cartoons. How about it?"

His eyes slid back and forth from my mother to me, as if they'd been oiled. His face was very shiny. His freckles looked like spots of paint that had been tossed across his nose. I could've kicked him.

"What's for dinner tonight?" I said.

My mother put away the mats in the drawer. She turned to look at me.

"Meat loaf," she said. "And baked potatoes and peas. And perhaps a pie for dessert."

Meat loaf for Polly.

"What kind of pie?" I said.

"Apple," she said very slowly and distinctly. "Does that suit you?"

Teddy let his tongue hang out of his mouth and practiced panting, like some kind of gross dog. Little drops of saliva dripped on the table top.

"Stop that!" I hollered. "You're disgusting!"

"Go brush your teeth," my mother said. "It's getting late."

"I already have," I said.

"So have I," Teddy said.

My mother looked at both of us.

"Don't push me," she said. "There's been enough aggravation around here already today. I don't need any more."

Teddy and I went to brush our teeth. He let me go first.

I wasn't going to say good-bye to her. Then I thought better of it and went out to the kitchen.

"Good-bye," I said in a stiff voice.

"Here's the money," she said, handing me two dollars. "Stop on your way home, will you? The freezer seems to be failing."

I took them. "What for?" I said.

"The ice cream," she said.

"I thought you said we were having pie."

She looked surprised. "I did," she said. "But don't you want vanilla ice cream to go with it? I figure, with Polly coming, we can spring for a little à la mode."

We smiled at each other.

"Yeah," I said, "a little à la mode is just the thing. Thanks, Mom."

chapter ten.

When I got downstairs, Al waved an envelope in my face. "Now hear this," she said. "Today is D day. I mail it today, no matter what. Neither rain nor snow nor sleet can stop me."

"That's pretty safe," I told her. "Considering it's June."

"And furthermore," she went on, ignoring me, "I may go on a cruise with my mother this summer. That's if Louise and my father don't come through with an invitation to visit them on the farm. My mother's thinking of going on a cruise to the West Indies. With a friend from Junior Miss fashions. She said she might take me."

"Cool," I said. "What do you do on a cruise?"

"You eat a lot," Al said. "And play shuffleboard, and they also have live entertainment and a swimming pool and dances. Lots of stuff like that."

"What happens if you get seasick?" I said.

She clapped her hand to her head. "Boy!" she said. "Trust you. Who else would think about being seasick when a friend says she might go on a cruise? Who else, I ask you? You're some killjoy is all I can say."

"I'm sorry," I said. "I didn't mean to be. It's just that I thought you might get seasick. And another thing. You want to be sure you don't go anywhere near the Bermuda Triangle." I looked at her. "Make sure before you pay your money."

Al looked puzzled. She almost always knows about things like the Bermuda Triangle.

"I read something about it but I can't remember what," she said.

I like having the upper hand now and then. Usually Al has it. This time it was me.

"Oh, you know," I said. "It's that place where the ships are sailing merrily along, happy as larks, and swoosh! all of a sudden, something swallows them up."

"Swallows the ship?" Al asked, incredulous.

I nodded. "That's right. It's very mysterious. People are always writing books about it and investigating. So far, nobody's come up with an answer. They think it might be a giant monster of the deep who's responsible. Either that or a sudden terrible storm that catches everyone unaware. Whatever it is, those ships are simply swept from the face of the earth. Nobody knows the answer," I finished in a low, brooding tone.

Al stomped along, stiff-legged.

"Hey," I said. "Slow down. You're going too fast."

Al stopped suddenly. I almost ran into her. "Next time I'm thinking of going on a cruise," she said, "you'll be the last person I tell. Forget I mentioned it. Just forget the whole thing. Boy."

She was in a huff for a while but she recovered. By the time we could see our school ahead, she said, "I wish there was some way I could get out of going to Nancy's tonight. I wish I hadn't said I'd go. I didn't think you'd ask me with Polly coming and all."

"I told you the three of us would do stuff together," I said. "Lots of stuff."

"I could make up an excuse," Al said.

"You mean you could lie," I said. "What'd you go to Nancy's for in the first place? You're always saying she's a first-class conformist. I thought you didn't like conformists."

"Once in a while you have to give one a chance," Al said. "You never can tell. I thought Nancy had possibilities. Did I tell you what she wanted to be when she grew up?"

"Yeah," I said.

Al shrugged. "You win some, you lose some," she said. "I guess the world is big enough for us to dwell in harmony with conformists. There's really nothing wrong with them." She didn't sound as if she were convinced that what she was saying was true.

When we got to our home room, Mr. Keogh was in a bad mood. Usually he's jolly and cheerful. He's almost never cross. Today was different.

"Come to order, all of you!" he shouted, slamming his hand down flat on the desk. "There'll be double homework over the weekend if you can't all pay attention, starting now!"

Martha Moseley raised her hand.

"Yes, Martha," Mr. Keogh said. "What is it?"

Martha stood up, clearing her throat.

"I can't do double homework this weekend, no matter what, Mr. Keogh," she said. "I'm going to my cousin's Sweet Sixteen party."

"Oh, la-di-da!" someone in the back said. "Oh, la-di-da-di-da!" People began to titter.

Martha took a long time sitting down. She smoothed her skirt carefully underneath her several times before she made it. Martha is bucking to play Scarlett O'Hara if they ever do a remake of *Gone With the Wind*.

"Silence!" Mr. Keogh roared. "One more disturbance and you've had it. Open your books and read the chapter on World War II, beginning on page ninety-five. I have prepared a test for you to take after you've finished reading. You will be allowed one half hour to complete everything, so there's no time to waste."

Everybody looked at everybody else. A couple of kids groaned. Mr. Keogh stood there, steam coming out of his ears. One thing about somebody who doesn't get mad often—when they do, watch out. Just don't mess with them. Mr. Keogh meant what he said.

When you think about it, World War II was very interesting. I know it seems as if it'd happened a long time ago, but it wasn't all that long. My mother and father were both little kids. My grandfather has told me about ration books and blackouts and about a German submarine landing on the beach on Long Island.

We have two Japanese kids in our class. Mr. Keogh read aloud to the class about the bombing of Pearl Harbor. They both got red and looked embarrassed. It wasn't their fault. Everybody knows that. But I guess they feel as if it were. I have some German blood, due to the fact my mother's mother was German. That doesn't make me responsible for Hitler. You have to think about things like that. The world is a very complex place. I sometimes think if I was going to school in Japan and they read about the Americans dropping the atomic bomb on Hiroshima, I'd be embarrassed too. So there you are.

The test wasn't all that bad. I'm a pretty fast

reader, so I finished the chapter and the test before the time limit. When I was through, I looked over at Al. She was slumped on her desk, staring into space. First she'd write something, then erase. Then write again. I thought she was having a rough time, although she usually finishes tests before me. This time she was still writing when Mr. Keogh announced it was time to hand in the papers.

Then I saw what she'd been working on. It was her letter. She must've finished her test way ahead of me and started to rewrite her letter to Brian. I figured if it ever got off the ground, that letter would be the most carefully worded document since the Declaration of Independence.

chapter eleven.

"Guess what?" Al said. "My invite to Nancy's doesn't include chow."

"That's weird," I said. Usually when people invite you to sleep over, they mean for dinner too. "I guess Nancy isn't as much of a conformist as you thought. No dinner, I mean."

Al looked thoughtful. "Maybe. Either that or her mother's on a really strict food budget. She says she's got lots of stuff stashed away for when her mother and father go to sleep. Potato chips, marshmallows, cheese. I didn't have the heart to tell her I don't eat junk food."

"You don't?"

"You know I've conquered my weakness," Al said sternly. "Just don't tempt me, that's all. Carrot sticks, celery, yum yum." Al sucked in her cheeks and her stomach at the same time. She really *did* look a lot thinner when she did that. She smiled her phony model's smile at me.

"How do you like my new custom-made jodhpurs?" she asked, bending her knee and putting her hands on her hips. "My tailor said I had the perfect shape for jodhpurs. 'Madam,' he said, 'you certainly are divinely slim in those jodhpurs.' "

Suddenly Al said in her normal voice, "If it's all right with your mother, I could come for supper at your house tonight, before I go to Nancy's. My mother has to go to a testimonial dinner for the head buyer in her department. She thought I wasn't going to be home so she didn't get anything for me to eat. There's stuff in the freezer, as usual," Al said. "I can eat that if your mother says no. There's lots of good stuff in our freezer."

"Sure you can come," I said.

"You better ask," Al said. "Your mother might not have enough to go around."

"OK, I'll check."

"You know something? Sometimes I wish my mother would settle down," she blurted out. "I'd feel better about her if she'd settle down. Suppose she's still having dates when I go to college?"

"Well," I said, "she'll be a lot older then. I mean,

you're not even in high school yet. Maybe she'll be tired of having dates by then. People don't go on having dates forever, after all."

"Look at your grandfather," Al said. "He still does and, pardon the expression, he's no spring chicken."

She was right. My grandfather is in his seventies and he still takes out women. He brought a lady named Mrs. Oakley over a while back and Teddy sang a dirty song in front of her. We haven't seen Mrs. Oakley since. She's probably still in shock. My grandfather laughed until tears ran down his cheeks. My father looked amused. My mother looked as if Teddy had just let out a huge burp. Or worse. Al and I hid in the broom closet.

"Did it occur to you," I said, "that your mother might not want to get married again?"

Al nodded. "I'm way ahead of you," she said. "Right after I came home from my father's wedding, I put it to her straight. 'Mom,' I said, 'what are your plans for the future?' "

Al's voice trailed off and she contemplated the ceiling. I waited. She kept looking at the ceiling. Finally I said, "Are you going to tell me what she said or do I have to guess?"

"She said, 'I live each day as it comes. I don't make plans. I've discovered it's best not to.' " Al looked at me. Then she began to roll her eyes in circles, first to the right, then to the left. She was doing her eye exercises. If she does them often enough, her eye muscles will get stronger and she won't have to wear glasses any more. Contact lenses make her nervous.

"Love me, love my glasses," Al says, but I don't think she means it.

"I have to go to a meeting of the *PeepHole*," Al said. That's the school literary magazine. "That is such a dumb name for a literary magazine it gives me warts," Al said. "I'll call you when I get home. Check with your mother, all right? About dinner?"

"Sure," I said. "But it'll be all right."

At the door she turned.

"Nancy says they have hot cereal every morning for breakfast. She says her mother makes it with quite a lot of lumps in it, and if I don't want to eat it we can just flush it down the toilet when she's not looking."

Al looked very depressed.

"I didn't know people ate hot cereal in warm weather. It's bad enough in winter. I mean, you expect it in winter. You're prepared, lumps and all. But summer." She shook her head.

"You could tell them your mother expects you home for breakfast," I said. "Tell them your mother doesn't like to eat breakfast alone."

"Yeah," Al said darkly. "I expect they'd buy that."

"It's worth a try," I said. "And look at it this way. If they have lumpy hot cereal for breakfast, it's just as well your invite didn't include dinner. Think of what they might have for dinner."

75

Al looked thoughtful.

"You are becoming a sage," she said. "I would never have thought it. But you're right. Just think." She wiped her forehead. "Man, that was close."

"Did you mail it yet?" I said.

"Not yet. I figured I'd wait until I got home and checked today's mail," Al said.

She raised both hands with the thumbs tucked under. "Banzai," she said.

I wouldn't be surprised if she waited one more day. To mail the letter, I mean.

chapter twelve.

Polly brought my mother a beautiful box that had been handmade in India. It said so on the bottom. There were yellow and blue birds on the top and then the box was coated with lacquer.

"Oh, it's lovely, Polly," my mother said, her eyes shining, after she'd unwrapped her present. "So lovely, Polly. I do thank you. I'll treasure it."

"My mother picked it out," Polly said. "She wanted to give you something to express her thanks for having me. She spent a lot of time looking for just the right thing. She thought you'd like it."

"I do, I do!" my mother crooned. She set the box

on the top of the hall cabinet which reaches almost to the ceiling.

"Why don't you girls take Polly's things into the bedroom and get settled? Teddy, you come with me." My mother propelled Teddy gently but firmly with her. "I could use some help in the kitchen."

Teddy was going to be a problem. I hadn't counted on that. All of a sudden I could see he would, however. He liked Polly a lot. He was going to include himself in everything we did.

"I want to go with them," I could hear him whine. Then he said in his usual penetrating voice, "Did she bring me anything? How come she brought you a present and not me? That's not fair."

I was showing Polly where she could hang her clothes, and the bureau drawers that I'd cleared for her, when I remembered something.

"Back in a sec," I said and raced into the kitchen. "Mom, is it all right if Al comes for supper? I told her it was. She's going to sleep over at Nancy's house but the invitation didn't include dinner so I said she could come here. OK?"

My mother looked annoyed.

"I wish you'd asked me first," she said. "You really shouldn't invite people for meals without making sure we have adequate food."

"It's only Al, Mom," I said. "If there's not enough, she'll sit and watch us eat. She just likes being here.

Anyhow, I can give her half of mine. She likes meat loaf."

"It's stew," my mother said.

"I thought you said meat loaf."

"Stew meat was on special. I guess I can always add a few carrots and potatoes."

"You're a good woman," I told her.

"How come she gets to have two friends for supper and I can't have even one?" Teddy said.

"Al and Polly are your friends too," my mother told him.

That took the starch out of Teddy. "They are?" he said, surprised.

"Certainly."

"Does that mean Hubie's her friend too?" he asked, pointing to me.

"You bet. I'll sleep in Hubie's top bunk any day," I said.

"I don't think he'd like that. He's not all that hot on girls," Teddy said.

"You want me to set the table now?" I asked, starting to get out the silver.

"It's a bit early, but if you like."

I took out the best linen napkins and matching mats. I wanted the best for Polly. Polly was used to nice things. Al didn't care that much, but Polly did. Besides, I figured if I dolled up the table enough, Polly wouldn't notice we were having stew.

"Can I help?" Polly said.

Just then Al rang her special ring. I opened the door. Polly hugged Al until Al got red in the face with pleasure. For such a skinny kid, Polly's pretty strong.

"I didn't recognize you without your apron on," Al said to Polly. Polly cooks a lot and always wears a huge apron.

"How goes it?" Al asked. She felt shy all of a sudden, I think. "You're hanging around here for a while, huh?"

Polly nodded. "Isn't that super? I'm so glad to be here with you all. We'll have a blast."

"I just stopped by for a sec," Al said.

"Mom said you could stay for chow," I told her.

Teddy sprang out from behind a chair. "She was mad," he said. "She said she'd have to throw in a few carrots and potatoes in case there wasn't enough."

"Let's go into my room," I said. "So we can have some privacy."

We zapped inside and I closed the door with a bang. I could hear Teddy breathing at the keyhole so I stuffed it with a sock.

"OK," I said, sitting on the bed. "Let's talk."

"Let Polly," Al said. She must not have gotten a letter or she'd want to go first.

"Tell us about Thelma," I said. I'd been dying to hear about Thelma.

"Two earth-shattering things have happened to

Thelma since I last saw you. One," Polly said, "is that she got a permanent. She looks as if she stuck her finger into an electric socket and the current got to her hair. Two—" Polly paused for effect. "Two is that she's carrying on a correspondence with a boy at a prep school. I think he might be her cousin. She forgot she told me her cousin was going to this same school. Anyway, now she says he's dreamy and stuff like that."

"Thelma says 'dreamy'?" I said. "She's in bad shape." Al didn't say anything.

"That's what you think," Polly said significantly. "She's wearing a bra and it's the real McCoy, not any training jazz."

We sat and pondered the mysteries of life for a minute.

Polly continued. "Thelma gets about three letters a week from this kid. I've seen his picture, and believe me, he's nothing to write home about. You know what it is." Polly poked a finger at us. "It's the friends. He has friends, and they're not her cousin. Plus they might be better looking. She says he's going to invite her up to his school for their fall dance. So naturally, Thelma's hanging on for dear life and writing up a storm, waiting for fall.

"Knowing Thelma," Polly went on, "it will come as no surprise to learn that she's become an expert on writing letters to boys." She fluttered her eyelashes. I didn't look at Al.

"She gives advice to any and all who ask," Polly said. "As a matter of fact, they don't have to ask. Thelma is a mine of unsolicited advice. Even if the conversation isn't about writing letters to boys, Thelma always manages to turn it around. You could be talking about a math test or a movie you saw, and in the flick of an eye Thelma will say, 'That reminds me of the last letter I got from Ron.' That's his name, Ron. Short for Ronald." Polly paused to let this sink in.

"False friends are everywhere," Polly said. "And Thelma is surrounded. Is she ever surrounded! At the moment there's nothing they won't do for her. But you wait. If she and the mysterious Ron aren't still pen pals come the fall, Thelma will be singing a different tune. You mark my words."

Polly smiled at us. "That's enough about Thelma. Tell me what's been happening around here. Anything new and startling?"

"Are you kidding?" Al said. "Same old junk."

"How about that kid you met at your father's wedding?" Polly asked her. "Did you ever hear from him?"

A thick silence, like a tent that had been dropped from the ceiling, fell over Al. Her face closed in on itself.

I answered for her. "Not yet," I said. "But she will. Tell her about the cruise, Al," I said.

"Polly doesn't want to hear about some dumb old cruise," Al said.

"Sure I do," Polly said. "Tell me."

Al sat, silent.

"She might go on a cruise with her mother," I said.

"Hey, it's too bad you didn't get to go to Africa, Polly," Al said in a phony gay voice. "That would've been so terrific if you'd gone with your parents. I saw a documentary film about the game preserves in Kenya. You can walk around practically touching the wild animals on one of those game preserves. That's my idea of something really special. Not like some dumb old cruise."

"I've never been on a cruise," Polly said. I didn't say anything. Everybody knew *I'd* never been anywhere.

"A friend of mine went on one with her mother and father, and she said it was terrific," Polly went on. "They went ashore at every port and saw the sights and shopped up a storm and had a wonderful time. She loved it. I think going on a cruise would be fun. That's neat, Al, that you're going."

"Only if I don't go to visit my father," Al said. "He might have me stay with him and Louise and the boys. They said something about me coming to visit at the wedding, but I haven't heard anything definite. They must've forgotten. Either that or something else came up. You know how things can come up and change everybody's plans. That happens all the time. Maybe they've had a change in plans."

"There's lots of time for you to hear from your father," I said. "School isn't out yet."

My mother knocked on the door. "Why don't you girls come out and say hello to Dad?" she said. "He just got home, and I think he'd like to see you all."

Usually when Al comes over, my father jumps up and says, "And who's this young lady?" as if he's never met her before. He shakes her hand and bows and clicks his heels. He's done this about a million times. Al loves it.

This time my father was settling down in his chair with his paper. He stood up and said, "Well, well, and how is the pride of West End Avenue?" to Polly. "I bet the neighborhood isn't the same with you in residence. How are you bearing up?"

You might know. Today, of all days.

"Dad," I said, "here's a friend of yours."

"Oh, hello, Al. How's the girl?" my father said, and went back to teasing Polly.

Al looked down at the rug, scuffling her shoes around for a minute. She lifted her head and watched my father and Polly joke around. Her hands hung down at her sides as if they didn't belong to her. I felt like pinching my father to make him notice Al. He should make a fuss over her today. She needed a fuss made over her.

"Dinner's about ready," my mother said. "Polly, will you sit here." She indicated the seat next to my father. The seat of honor.

"And, Al, will you sit here, next to Teddy, please."

Next to Teddy. That was like being invited to the White House and landing next to Amy.

In the end, it turned out all right. We had a good time. My mother and father had wine and we had milk and we drank a toast to Polly's visit. Al smiled and talked a lot. There was enough stew and the pie was delicious. And the à la mode.

Al helped clear the table.

"I hate to eat and run," she told my mother, "but I've got to go now. They're expecting me at Nancy Bishop's. Thank you for another lovely dinner."

Something in her voice must've gotten to my mother because she stopped what she was doing and put her arms around Al. Al wasn't the kind of person you put your arms around for no reason.

"It was so nice to have you, Al," my mother said. "You're always welcome here. You're like one of the family."

"I am?" Al said, amazed.

"Yes, you are," my mother said.

Teddy hit himself on his forehead. "Oh, no!" he cried. "Not another sister!" but he didn't sound sad.

Al looked dazed. "One of the family," she muttered to herself. I heard her.

I walked to the door with her and waited while she

made sure she had her key. She had to go back to her apartment to get her stuff.

"It was cool," she said. "Everything was. Thank your mother again for me."

"Sure," I said. "Have a good time at Nancy's."

I walked to her apartment door with her.

"Want me to come in with you?" I said.

"No, you better get back," she said. "Polly will be waiting for you. I just have to pick up my pajamas and my toothbrush."

"See you tomorrow," I said. "Eat a few lumps of hot cereal for me."

Al did a few bumps and grinds to show me she was all right. "You know what Nancy wants to do when I get there?" she said.

"No. What?"

"She wants us to practice kicking. You know. She practices her Rockette routine every night before she goes to bed. To stay in shape in case the Rockettes are still going strong by the time she gets old enough to join them."

Al gave me the owl eye. Not the bilious eye, the owl eye. They're different.

I didn't know what to say.

"Far out," I said.

"Yeah," she said. "See you," and she zapped inside for her stuff.

chapter thirteen.

"You should've warned me," Polly said, snuggling underneath the covers. My mother had borrowed a cot from a friend for her to sleep on. The room was pretty crowded. We'd manage.

"About what?"

"Not to say anything to Al. You know. About whether she'd gotten a letter from that kid she met. I got the bad vibes. The minute I asked, I got the vibes. They practically rattled my teeth, they were so strong. If I'd known it was a sore subject, I wouldn't have said anything. You should've warned me," she repeated.

"I didn't think," I said. "How did I know you were

going to start in telling about Thelma and how she was an expert on letter writing to boys. That was some timing is all I can say. Al's been agitating every day that goes by and she doesn't hear from either Brian or her father and Louise. She thinks the world has deserted her."

"We could try thought waves," Polly said slowly.

"How do you do that?"

"Well, you say slowly and carefully, 'Write to Al, write to Al.' You have to concentrate on the people you're sending the waves to. You have to say their names over and over inside your head. That's so the thought waves know where they're supposed to go.

" 'Write to Al, write to Al.' You have to say it about a thousand times. To be on the safe side. Then, if it works, the people you're sending the waves to will drop whatever it is they're doing and say, 'I must write to Al!' as if they'd thought of it themselves."

"Does it work?" I asked.

Polly shrugged. "Sometimes." She yawned. "Anyway, it's worth a try. It doesn't cost anything." She turned on her side and pulled the blanket over her head.

"Boy, am I tired," she said.

"You can't go to sleep now!" I cried. "Not on your first night! We've got loads of things to discuss."

"Go ahead." Polly's voice seemed to be growing fainter and fainter. "I'm listening."

I started to tell her about Martha Moseley on ac-

88

count of Polly is a charter member of the anti-Martha club.

"Her cousin's having this Sweet Sixteen party," I began, "and . . ."

Polly shot up in bed, forgetting she was tired. "Sweet Sixteen party!" she shouted. "You're kidding me! You've got to be kidding me. The Sweet Sixteen routine went out with high shoes and starched dresses, for Pete's sake!"

"Tell Martha that," I said, glad I had her attention. "She's acting as if her cousin had just been picked to be the first female to go into space. Anyway, her cousin's got this strapless dress."

Polly sank back into bed. She put her hand to her head. "What hath God wrought?" she asked me and herself. I knew she didn't expect an answer so I didn't give her one. Even if I had one.

"Yes," I said. "Also, the club where the party's being held is going to be decorated like a disco. Strobe lights, the works."

Polly closed her eyes. "Keep talking," she said. "I'm listening with my eyes closed."

I told Polly about my dream. About Mr. Richards dancing with Martha in her cousin's dress and then how her cousin tried to rip off the dress and how Al came into the dream and said Martha would never get a letter from a boy unless she signed it 'Your old pal, Al' and Martha said her name wasn't Al and Al said, 'That's neither here nor there.' "

89

I love that story. Every time I tell it, it gets better. "And then," I said, "you'll never guess what happened next. Next morning when Al and I were going to school, she said she'd had a dream about Mr. Richards too. The same exact night. Isn't that bizarre?"

I heard a little buzzing sound coming from Polly's bed. But I was so absorbed in my story that at first I didn't pay any attention. It sounded like a mosquito. A very small mosquito.

I looked over at Polly. She was asleep. With her mouth open. The buzzing sound came from her. She was snoring.

Boy.

I turned off the light. How about that. I must be a pretty boring storyteller.

Oh, well. There was always tomorrow.

chapter fourteen.

The new assistant super's kids were lurking behind the dryers when Polly and I took the wash down to the laundry room Saturday morning.

They sort of made a career out of lurking.

"Hi," I said. "How's it going?"

"What's it to you?" came the reply.

"Cute kid," Polly said. "Very cute."

"They're very smart," I said in a loud voice. "They're so smart you wouldn't believe it."

There was a silence while they figured their next move. The littlest one, named Clorinda, stuck out her head and her tongue at the same time.

"If I were you," Polly said, "I'd see a doctor. How

long has your tongue been that peculiar color?"

Clorinda disappeared. We could hear them whispering to one another.

"I wonder if I remembered to take the money out of my pocket before I put my jeans in," I said. "You kids want to watch the machine for me and put the stuff in the dryer if I'm not back when the washer stops?"

The middle one, who sometimes smiled if she wasn't careful, popped out.

"I don't mind," she said.

"Terrific. I'll be back in half an hour." At the door Polly and I turned quickly. We caught them all staring at us over the tops of the washers. Clorinda opened her mouth, thought better of whatever it was she had in mind, and closed it.

We waved at them.

"Don't take any wooden nickels," Polly said. On our way upstairs we decided to stop and see if Al was back yet. I rang and waited. No one answered.

"I guess she's not home yet," I said. We were halfway down the hall when Al's mother opened the door.

"Oh, it's you, dear," she called. "Come in for a minute, why don't you? I expect Alexandra back momentarily."

"I thought you were at work," I said. "I wouldn't have rung if I'd known you were here." I didn't mean that the way it sounded.

"I took the day off," she said. She wore a pretty robe with roses on it and her face was clean. I don't mean it isn't usually, but she wears a lot of make-up—eye shadow and all. She has to be constantly chic, being in Better Dresses, and that isn't easy.

"It's a strain on my mother," Al had told me. "Always being at her best. You try it sometime."

I would never try it. Not ever.

"You remember Polly Peterson," I said. "She's staying at our house for two weeks while her mother and father are in Africa."

"Africa!" Al's mother said. "I've always wanted to go there. How marvelous for them. Come in and have some coffee or tea."

We each had a cup of tea and some cinnamon toast. Al's mother doesn't do a lot of cooking, but she makes good cinnamon toast. I'll say that for her.

Ever since I spent some time alone with Al's mother while Al was at her father's wedding, I've felt comfortable with her. Before that, she made me nervous. I think she's lonely. Otherwise, why would she ask Polly and me in on a Saturday morning?

We talked about a lot of things. She told us a couple of funny stories about when Al was little. We were laughing when the telephone rang.

"Let it go," she said. We sat there and drank our tea. The phone kept ringing. Finally she answered.

"Yes," she said, "I decided to take the day off. Oh, that sounds lovely. I think it would be all right. Let me call you back, though. My daughter isn't home and I want to check with her first. I'll call you the minute she gets back."

We got up to go. Never wear out your welcome, my mother says. Al's mother saw us to the door. The mail was lying on the hall table.

"Nothing interesting," she said.

I couldn't resist.

"Did Al get a letter?" I said.

"From her father, do you mean?" She leafed through the pile. "Nothing here for her. Just bills."

Maybe she didn't know about Brian.

The elevator stopped and Al got off. "Don't tell me," she said, taking us in, "you're having a protest meeting."

"How was it?" I said.

Al put down her bag. "Ta-da!" she said. "And now we present the Rockettes! Let's have a big hand for a bunch of really keen little girls!"

And she started kicking.

"Really, Alexandra," her mother said. She couldn't help laughing, though.

When Al ran out of steam, she stopped.

"How come you're home today, Mom?" she said.

"When I woke up, I was tired so I called the store and told them not to expect me," her mother said.

"Do you feel all right?" Al asked.

"Perfectly. Last night was rather late, that's all. If

94

you ladies don't mind, I'll excuse myself and go take a tub," she said.

"Thanks for the tea," Polly said. "It was delicious."

"And the cinnamon toast," I said, "which was even more delicious."

Al said proudly, "She makes good cinnamon toast, doesn't she?" She looked at the mail in her mother's hand.

"Anything for me?" she said.

Her mother shook her head. "Not today," she said.

"Not any day," Al replied.

"Hey, Al," I said hurriedly, "want to come with Polly and me to see the Egyptian room at the Metropolitan? They say it's cool."

"You never go to museums on your own," Al said. "This must be Polly's influence. A little culture is a dangerous thing, methinks."

Teddy came out into the hall.

"There you are, Ted," Polly said, as if she'd spent half the morning looking for him. "Want to come with us to the museum to see some mummies?"

"Mummies?" Teddy said. He looked suspicious. He figured there must be a catch if he was being included. "That's what my friend Hubie calls his mother. Mummy."

"I hope Hubie's mummy doesn't look like the ones we're going to see," Al said. "They've been dead for years."

"Go ask your mother," Polly directed. "We'll wait here."

"What'd you do that for?" I asked when Teddy had raced back inside to get permission.

"Why not? He's a perfectly good kid."

"That's what you think."

"Give him a break. You were a child once yourself," Polly reminded me.

"Do they have belly dancing in this Egyptian room?" Al asked. "My belly dancing is getting stale. I could use a refresher course."

Teddy came running back. "She says it's OK. I told her Polly asked me to go. She said that was nice of Polly." Teddy put his hand in Polly's and smiled at her. He never did that to me.

"Alexandra," Al's mother said, "if you'd come in for a minute, I'd like to talk to you. Just for a minute. Have a good time, all of you," she said and went inside.

Polly and I zapped down to the laundry room to get the clothes. Teddy tagged along. Give that kid an inch, he always takes a mile. Only one washing machine was churning. The dryers were empty. I listened. The lurkers had gone.

So had the clothes.

"The only stuff that'll fit them will be Teddy's," I said. "They can probably wear his shirts and pants. Maybe his socks. But that's it."

"How about my underwear?" Teddy asked.

"Girls don't wear boys' underwear," I said.

"Girls? Yikes!" Teddy leaped straight up in the air.

But it was all right. When we got upstairs, my mother told us Clorinda and her sisters had delivered the laundry. "She said," my mother reported, "to tell you that there wasn't no money. Your girl must've taken all her money out of her pockets, Clorinda said. But look." My mother held up a few items. "Just behold." I must've put in my new red shirt by mistake. All the white things were tinged with pink.

"Nothing your father likes better than pink underwear."

"How can I go to gym wearing pink underwear?" Teddy wailed.

Al's special ring broke that up. "The secret is, Ted," Polly told him, "to pretend you're Superman and it's his suit you're wearing under your clothes. That way you'll be proud of what you've got on, and pretty soon all your friends will want underwear just like yours."

Teddy put his hands in his pockets to show how blasé he was, how accustomed to standing around in a roomful of girls on his way to the museum. He made slits of his eyes to show how thoughtful he was. Huge, deep thoughts were skittering around inside that tiny head of his.

"Maybe," he said. "But I doubt it."

We all piled into the elevator.

"My mother's got a date with a man named Mr. Wright tonight," Al said.

There was a silence as she gave us a piercer.

"So?" I said.

"Mr. Right," Al said slowly, giving us another piercer. "Haven't you ever heard of Mr. Right?"

Polly and I looked at each other. Teddy scratched his stomach.

"You know," Al said impatiently. "In the olden days girls sat around on the front porch, knitting and stuff, waiting for Mr. Right to come along. That's spelled R-I-G-H-T. The one and only. Everybody has a Mr. Right waiting somewhere out there in this great big wonderful world of ours." She spread wide her hands and clipped Teddy on the side of the head.

He yelped

"Sorry," she said.

"So what if this guy spells his name W-R-I-G-H-T? It's pronounced the same way. What's the dif? I think it's a sign," Al continued as we hit the street. "She's finally found her Mr. Right. Or Mr. Wright. Whatever he calls himself. It's definitely a sign."

Teddy ran ahead of us and waited at the corner. I could tell by the way he was hitching up his pants that he was feeling important. He hoped he'd run into some of his friends so he could tell them he was going to the Metropolitan to see the mummies.

"I didn't know your mother knew how to knit," Polly said.

"She doesn't," Al answered. "And I don't need to tell you we don't have a front porch, either."

We all had a good laugh about that. Then we passed a mailbox.

"Did you or didn't you?" I asked Al.

She shook her head and held up her fists. Both thumbs were tucked under. She kept them that way until we got to the museum.

chapter fifteen.

"It's like a feather bed," Al sighed, luxuriating in the comfort of the sleeping bag. When she stretched out full length, her head was partly in the closet. My room *was* pretty small.

"We could take turns," Polly offered.

"Nope," Al said. "I don't want to share."

I went to get us some eats. Teddy's room was dark. My mother and father were at the movies. I got us each a carton of yogurt. When I went back, I closed the door behind me. In case Teddy was seized with a desire to walk in his sleep. He sometimes does. Mostly when I have guests sleeping over. It gives him a good excuse for wandering outside my room and eavesdropping. Teddy is nothing if not transparent.

When we finished our snack, I pulled out from under my bed the box of dress-ups I've been collecting for some time. My mother gave me some stuff she doesn't want any more. Al's mother contributed a pair of lounging pajamas she bought on sale that didn't fit. "Beware of bargains that don't fit," she told me. There were some other things from my aunt and a couple of other ladies.

We had three pairs of high-heeled shoes. Al got to wear the ones with the backs cut out because her feet were the biggest. Mine fit me perfectly. Polly stuffed tissue paper in the toes of hers. We were all set.

I heard a noise at the door. I opened it a crack. Sure enough. Teddy was on his rounds. He even stuck out his hands in front of him the way sleepwalkers are supposed to do. I could see his eyes shining behind his half-closed lids. Who did he think he was kidding?

"Hey," I whispered loudly, "Teddy's walking in his sleep. They say the best way to wake a sleepwalker is to throw a bucket of cold water over him." I winked at Al and Polly. Teddy stopped dead in his tracks. Then he turned slowly and began walking back to his room.

"Quick," I said. "Fill the pitcher with water. I'll get some ice cubes to make it really cold."

Teddy was practically running by the time he got to his room. He hurled himself under the covers.

I looked down at him. "It's OK," I called. "He's asleep. Just keep the water handy in case."

We rolled around on the floor for about five minutes, holding our stomachs and laughing. I made them put pillows over their mouths so Teddy wouldn't hear. He'd probably stick his head in the door and say, "What's so funny?" forgetting he was supposed to be asleep. He's very hard to squelch.

After a while we got down to brass tacks.

"Dibs on the purple passion," Al said, grabbing for the dress my aunt had made to wear to her senior prom. She'd spent a lot of time and money making that dress. She was pretty good at sewing, she thought. She bought a pattern and everything. It was a sexy dress. It had a slinky skirt and a top so tight it almost cut off her circulation, "like a tourniquet," she told me. Anyway, at the final fitting, it didn't look so hot. One side was perfect. The other side sloped.

My aunt is pretty old. Somewhere in her thirties. But even after all that time, she still sort of cried when she told me about that dress. She laughed a lot too, but I could see moisture in her eyes.

"It was so awful," she said, dabbing away. "So ghastly." So her mother bought her a white organdy or some such turkey and she threw the purple one in a dark corner of her closet and found it years later when she was cleaning. Then she sent it to me.

Al loves that dress. She's worn it so often she knows

102

where all the safety pins are located and how to work the zipper, which is on its last legs.

After some deliberation between my mother's first present from my father—a hostess gown printed with huge orange and black flowers—and a black velvet bathrobe someone had donated, Polly whipped into the bathrobe. It was so big she disappeared momentarily. Just when we thought we'd lost her, she stuck out her head and smiled.

"Black suits you," Al said solemnly.

I wore a dress I had when I was eight. The skirt came about to where my underwear ended but the rest fit me fine, which ought to give you some idea of my shape.

Then I made everybody up. I was best at that. I took out my shoe box filled with cosmetics. I had a bunch of stuff I fished out of my mother's wastebasket, plus some junk I bought at the five-and-ten.

"Stand still," I told Al as I went to work. I worked a long time on her. I wouldn't let her check in the mirror. "When I'm finished," I told her. "Hang on to your glasses so they don't get lost."

"This is a lot of baloney," she grumbled. "You're hiding the real me."

I gave her a piercer. "Is that all bad?" I said. She shut up. When I was done, I let her look at herself.

"Wild," she said, "absolutely wild. I look like Groucho Marx," but I could tell she was pleased.

Right off the bat, Polly got some mascara in her

eye. She carried on like a maniac, rushing to wash her face. She wouldn't let me put any more stuff on her. "I'm a natural beauty, anyway," she said.

Polly was Carole Lombard. She was always Carole Lombard. She had even bought a cigarette holder at a tag sale which she whipped around as if she used it every day. She'd seen every one of Carole's movies on the Late Late Show. Polly didn't have a curfew. Her mother and father trusted her. Which is why she sees all those neat old movies on the Late Late Show. She also has bags and circles under her eyes frequently, but that's beside the point.

"Philip, darling," Polly cooed, "you simply must wear that ascot I gave you to the Fordyces' ball. You'll be the hit of the evening. Every woman in the room will want you to dance with her." She waved the cigarette holder in my face. "I do hope Sonny doesn't make a scene when he sees us together." She turned to Al and me. "Sonny is my first husband. He's very jealous. He has had five wives. He collects wives the way other men collect stamps." Polly fluttered her eyelashes until I swear I could feel a draft.

When she'd finished, Al tottered to her feet. Her shoes had the highest heels of all.

"Your behind wiggles," I said.

"It's supposed to," she said. "Marilyn's does. On her it looks good."

"Marilyn?" Polly said. "Who's she?"

"Take off your glasses before you start," I told Al.

104

"How do you expect Polly to know who you are with those glasses on?"

"I can't see without them," Al complained, but she took them off anyway.

Suddenly she bent both knees and peered near-sightedly over her shoulder at us, smiling, running her hands up and down her sides.

"Now do you know?" I asked Polly.

"You got me," Polly said.

"OK," Al said, "I guess I have to bring out the heavy artillery." She broke into "Diamonds Are a Girl's Best Friend." She knew all the words, all the motions Marilyn made when she sang that song. She should. She'd watched it often enough on the tube.

"Pear shaped or square shaped," Al's voice soared as she leaped around the room. When she quit, exhausted, Polly and I both clapped.

"That was really good," Polly said. "You were terrific. You were Marilyn Monroe, right?"

"Good girl, Pol," I told her.

I hate being last. I get nervous. But it was my turn now.

"You've got to imagine me as a tiny tot on a southern plantation," I told them.

"*C'est impossible*," Polly said.

"*Nyet*," came from Al.

"Try," I commanded.

I did my Shirley Temple tap dance. We don't have stairs in our apartment, so I had to pile up some books and pretend they were stairs. I do this tap dance that Shirley did in one of her movies with Bill Robinson. They tap up and down the stairs. It's really great. However, it's not easy to tap dance in high heels. I stumbled and knocked down the pile of books. "How about a spot of caviar?" Polly said. "I haven't had any in ages. And a glass of white wine."

I got a jar of peanut butter and some saltines, plus a bottle of ginger ale. Our tongues stuck to the roofs of our mouths, due to the peanut butter.

"A spot of mayonnaise might be a good idea," Al said when she could speak.

"I think if Brian takes me to one more gourmet restaurant," she said, "I will expire. The dear boy has taken me to every gourmet restaurant in the city. You know what I want? Just one perfect hamburger. That's all. But dear Brian." She put the back of her hand against her forehead and sighed. "He's so generous. And so extravagant."

"I have this boyfriend named Philip," Polly said. "He wants to buy me a Jaguar."

"Who's Philip?" I said. "How come I never heard of him before?"

"He's this boy in my school," Polly said.

"You made him up," I said.

"I did not. He is this boy in my school," Polly said. "His family's very rich. He's lived a lot of different places, just like me. His parents are friends of my parents."

"How come you never mentioned him before?" I said.

Polly shrugged. "Why should I? He's just a boy. Our families might go skiing in Switzerland next Christmas."

"Oh, sure," Al said.

Polly looked surprised. "Why would I make that up?" she said. "Anyway"—she went back to her pretend voice—"he wants to buy me a Jag and I said, positively, absolutely not. If he wants, he can buy me a motorcycle, but a Jag, no."

"I'm tired," Al said. "I think I'll hit the sack." I looked at her to see if she was serious. She was.

"Boy," I said, "it's not even ten o'clock. How come you're crumpling so early?"

"It's been a tough day," Al said. Her head was in the closet so I couldn't see her face.

Polly and I looked at each other. It wasn't any fun with just the two of us. We might as well go to bed too.

I turned out the lights. I wasn't sleepy. I realized I still had all the junk on my face—lipstick, mascara, and eye shadow. My mother would kill me. The sheets would be covered with junk.

I sat up. "Hey," I said, "we better wash our faces. Otherwise we'll louse up the sheets. My mother will kill us."

Silence. No one answered. They couldn't have gone to sleep so fast.

A buzzing sound came from Polly's side of the room. This time it sounded like a really big mosquito.

"What's that?" Al said from the closet.

"I thought you were asleep," I said in a sour tone. "That's Polly. She snores."

"She snores?" Al said. "Holy Toledo. That's really something. I didn't know anybody our age snored. I thought only fathers snored. You mean you've got to put up with that noise for two whole weeks?" She sounded glad. "Boy, that'd sure drive me up the wall."

I had a feeling she was smiling in the dark.

chapter sixteen.

We usually have waffles Sunday morning. My father makes them. They're his specialty. He's very conceited about his waffles. They're good. I don't know if they're the best in the world, the way he says. But they *are* good.

I ate two and a half. Al only had one.

"I'm on a diet," she said.

Polly wanted jam instead of syrup on hers. I never heard of people eating jam on waffles. Teddy watched as Polly spread strawberry jam on her waffle.

"I want mine like hers," he said. He is famous for never trying anything new.

"Try mine," Polly said. She held out a piece on her fork.

Teddy got it up to his mouth. Then he chickened out. "I don't think I'd like it," he said, as if the whole thing had been Polly's idea.

"You're a creep," I whispered in his ear when my father wasn't looking.

Right after breakfast Al carried her dishes out to the kitchen. "I better split," she said. Sunday was togetherness day at Al's house. It was the only time her mother had to spend with her. They usually did something like going to a play or a movie or a concert.

"I wonder if Mr. Wright will tag along," Al said glumly. "Or maybe Ole Henry."

"I thought you said your mother was getting bored with Ole Henry," I said.

"I think she is. The problem is, will she clue Ole Henry in or will he have to figure it out for himself?" Al said. "One thing about Ole Henry is if he goes with us, we take a taxi. Ole Henry is a regular taxi freak. It's the one good thing about him. Usually he's a cheapskate. He's got a taxi fetish. He takes one even if he only has to go five blocks. My mother wouldn't take a taxi unless she was caught in a blizzard with a broken leg. Even then I'm not sure." She went out to thank my mother. Al never forgets to say thank you.

Polly folded her napkin neatly.

"I've got to get going," she said.

110

"Where are you going?" I said. "I thought we were going to do something today. I didn't know you had to go anywhere."

Polly looked surprised. "I told you. I've got to go to Thelma's to work on our history project. We have to do it together. Thelma said to come over for lunch and we'd work all afternoon. I told you that."

"I don't remember," I said. "I don't think you did."

"Yes, I did," Polly said firmly. "I know I did."

"I don't think you did."

"I might mail my letter today," Al said.

Polly frowned. "For Pete's sake, why don't you just go ahead and mail it?" she said. "All you do is talk about mailing it. Go ahead and mail it, mail the darn thing."

"Yeah," Teddy said, looking from Al to Polly. He always had to get into the act. "Why don't you go ahead and mail the dumb old letter anyway?" He looked around to make sure we were all paying attention.

"Mail the dumb thing," he repeated.

"That's enough," my father said. He was reading the Sunday papers and, as usual, I thought he didn't hear anything that went on around him. As usual, I was wrong.

"That's quite enough, Teddy," my father said.

I walked Al to the door. Her shoulders drooped.

"Have a good time with your mother," I said.

I opened our door.

Al said, "Do you think it's a dumb thing? My letter, I mean. Do you think it's dumb?"

"Of course not," I said.

"You wouldn't tell me even if you did," she said.

"Of course I would," I said.

Al lifted her head and looked at me. One thing about people who wear glasses is that it's hard sometimes to see their eyes and know what they are thinking.

"I don't know why I kid myself," she said.

"You don't kid yourself," I told her. "You never do."

She shook her head. "That's all you know," she said. "I kid myself all the time. See you," she said and walked down the hall to her apartment. She didn't use her key. She leaned on the bell and rang and rang until her mother opened the door.

"My word, Alexandra," she said, "you're making enough noise to wake the dead."

"Sorry, Ma," Al said. She went inside, and after a couple of minutes I went back inside my apartment and shut the door.

chapter seventeen.

"How was yesterday?" I asked Al next morning.

"Disaster," she said sadly.

"What happened?"

"Well, first thing," she said, ticking off on her fingers, "was when Ole Henry arrived unannounced right after I got home from your house. He was in a foul mood on account of he just had a fight with his mother."

"Ole Henry has a mother?" I said, amazed. To me, Ole Henry looks too old to have a mother. An alive mother, that is.

"Sure. She lives with her sister. Ole Henry supports her. He doesn't like his mother too much, I guess, but he feels guilty because he doesn't like her, so he goes to see her every other weekend. They fight a lot. She's always telling him what to do, and he resents it."

My gosh. If my mother is still telling me what to do when I'm as old as Ole Henry, I'm going to be very depressed, I can tell you. I thought when people grew up and had jobs and money in the bank and everything, their mothers didn't still tell them what to do. What's the good of getting old if you can't finally do what you want instead of what your mother wants you to? One of the main reasons I want to grow up is so I can go to bed when I feel like, instead of having her say, "Time for bed." That and "We'll see" are at the top of my hate parade.

"Second," Al went on, "when Henry got to our pad, he was hungry. So my mother made him a piece of toast to go with his coffee, and he said, 'Nothing sweet in the larder?' and I could feel her blood pressure rising. You know what she said?"

"No," I said. "What?"

Al started to laugh. "She said, 'Like it or lump it,' and went into her room and closed the door. So Ole Henry went into a snit but he ate the piece of toast and got himself another cup of coffee. He can't think on an empty stomach, I guess." Al gave me a shot of her bilious eye. "I was giving him the bilious eye behind his back, but I guess the rays weren't strong enough because they had no effect."

114

"Maybe he had on his bilious eye vest," I said.

Al looked puzzled. "What's that?" she said.

"You never heard of a bilious eye vest?" I said. "It's similar to a bulletproof vest. It wards off bilious eyes, that's all."

"Oh, you," Al said. "Anyway, after a couple of minutes Vi came out of her room and gave Ole Henry the mitten."

"What the heck did she do that for?" I said. "What good's one mitten, and why did she give him one when she doesn't like him any more?"

"That means they broke up," Al explained to me.

"They broke up?" I didn't know people Vi and Henry's age broke up, like teenagers. Weird. As a matter of fact, this whole conversation was weird.

"Why'd they do that?" I asked.

"I guess my mother's had it with him," Al said. "She said Ole Henry wasn't shooting for a permanent relationship. He's not the marrying kind any more on account of he's been married a few times and he's broke from paying alimony."

"Alimony?"

"The dough a divorced man has to pay his wife. Sometimes women have to pay their husbands alimony. But only if the husband gets to keep the kids."

Al is very well informed. She reads the papers every day and also goes to the library and reads all kinds of business magazines, although she says they're pretty boring, and sometimes she reads *The*

Wall Street Journal to find out what's going on in the financial world. She likes to keep all bases covered, she says.

"Did he mind when Vi gave him the mitten?" I asked.

"I don't think he broke down and wept," Al said in her super-sarcastic voice. "Vi says all he wanted anyway was a hot meal now and then and a place to rest his feet."

"How about that time you saw them kissing each other like they were on their way to the altar?" I asked her. Only a month or so ago Al was sure her mother and Ole Henry were going to get married and ask her to go to Bermuda with them on their honeymoon because they felt sorry for her being alone.

"Listen, I can't be right all the time," Al said. "Human relationships are subject to immediate change. Anyway, I guess that was just a friendly kiss. It didn't look like it but maybe it was. What's a kiss anyway?"

"How do I know?" I said. "If I know your mother, she'll find another boyfriend."

"Please," Al said. "We do not refer to the Ole Henrys of this world as 'boyfriends.' We call them 'beaux.' My mother can't abide the term 'boyfriend.' "

"OK. Maybe she'll find another beau, then."

"I hope so. She likes to go out at night, as you know. If there's one thing she can't stand, it's going out to dinner with a bunch of women who fight over who had the shrimp salad and who had the veal. Stuff like that. She says that's very embarrassing. She'd rather stay at home than do that."

"Maybe we could fix her up with the new math teacher," I said. "He's not married."

"The one with the red beard?" Al screwed up her face into a ball. "He's about twenty-six years old. My mother wouldn't be caught dead out with somebody practically young enough to be her son. I guess we'll have to put our money on this Mr. Wright. I like the sound of him."

We walked along for a while, not talking. At the corner Al turned to me.

"You know what I think? I think they changed their minds. They don't really want me to come visit. They shouldn't have asked me at all. They might even have turned the boys against me."

I knew she meant her father and Louise.

"Maybe they make fun of me behind my back. They probably say, 'Oh, that fat, dumb old Al. What's she doing in our family anyway? We don't want any fat, dumb old sister.'"

Al stumped down the sidewalk, her back stiff and straight. "Al," I said, running to keep up, "you know that's not so. You know perfectly well they don't feel that way. It's just that the mail is slow. Sometimes letters take a long time to get where they're supposed to go."

"What do you know?" Al turned on me. "You don't know squat about those people. One thing I say is it's cruel to invite people to come visit and then not to follow through. It's downright cruel. I don't care. I simply do not care."

Sometimes the walk to school seems short. Sometimes long. Very long. This was one of those mornings it seemed extra long. When we got to the bottom of the school steps, Al said in an angry voice, "And another thing. Don't ask me over again while Polly's there. At your house. I knew it wouldn't work. Two's company, three's a crowd, as they say. We'll just suspend our friendship until Polly leaves. If she ever does, that is."

"Don't think you have a priority on getting sore," I said. I felt like hitting her. "You're a royal pain, that's what you are. One big, fat royal pain." I shouldn't have called her big and fat. She has lost some weight but she's still sensitive. But the words came rushing out and I didn't stop them.

"If that's the way you feel, OK," I said. She kept going up the steps. "It's all right with me. You're probably right. You can't handle more than one friend at a time. That's your problem."

The words hung in the air.

At the top she turned.

"Don't forget Thelma," she said. "Old Thelma's hanging in there. Just don't forget her, that's all."

She disappeared inside.

If that was the way she wanted it, all right. Just a very big all right. I could get along without Al. If I had to. I walked up the steps very slowly, very carefully, so I wouldn't jostle the things running around inside my head.

Martha Moseley came down the hall, gesturing with her hands, holding her audience captive with her wondrous tales of the Sweet Sixteen party.

"Well, of course"—Martha pursed her mouth in that disgusting way she has—"he's a lot older. And so handsome he'd make you die. He said he'd write."

I wanted Al to be there. Mad as I was at her, I wished she were there to put Martha in her place. Al was an expert at putting Martha in her place. I racked my brain in the hope of coming up with a super Al-type put-down for Martha. Nothing came.

To my horror, the only thing I could think of to do was to put my thumbs in my ears and waggle my fingers at Martha. But the worst thing of all was that I stuck out my tongue. Even Teddy might've thought twice about doing such a dumb, childish thing. I was mortified.

I ran into the girls' room so I wouldn't hear them laughing at me. I ran a basin full of cold water and put my face down into it. It made me feel better. Not much. Only a little.

It was going to be a long day.

chapter eighteen.

My mother was lying down when I got home. The shades were pulled, the room as dark as night. That meant she had a migraine. That's a super terrible kind of headache that flattens her. I've noticed that when she gets one my father becomes very quiet and withdrawn. I think her headache and my father are connected. Most of the time my parents get along fine. But once in a while they fight. Last night I heard their voices rising and falling, angry voices. I was glad Polly had fallen asleep.

It seems odd to me that I can always tell the sound of an angry voice. I wasn't eavesdropping exactly. But I can always tell when they're fighting. Then there's a different atmosphere in the house. I wish I could open all the windows and push out the unfriendly stuff and let in lots of fresh air and sunlight and affection so we'd be back to our usual life. It's not that simple. After they fight, my mother and father walk around carefully, not touching each other, speaking with great politeness to one another, as if they were strangers on a train. If the fight's been bad, then my mother gets a migraine.

I'm glad my parents don't fight often. Just once in a while is bad enough. It's OK for me and Al to fight. Or me and Polly. I mean, we're kids. I don't like it when grownups fight. It's different, somehow. More serious. I think people should get over fighting by the time they're adults.

I peeked in at my mother lying in her dark room. Her arm was over her eyes.

"Can you manage without me?" she whispered. She must've heard me open the door. "Polly and you can get the dinner, I imagine."

"Don't worry about a thing," I told her.

"And try not to fight with Teddy," my mother said, turning on her side.

Human relationships are subject to immediate change. Al said that. She was right. One minute everything was hunky-dory, the next minute everything was topsy-turvy. Just when I thought I had two really good friends for life, it turned out I was wrong. One minute all was peace and harmony in our house, the next my mother had a migraine.

The telephone rang. It was Thelma.

"Hey, how are you?" she said. I didn't tell her. What business was it of hers how I was?

"Polly's not here," I said.

"I know. Just wanted to let her know that party I was talking to her about was definite. Tell her that, will you? Tell her I'll get back to her about her date. OK?" Thelma hung up. Get back to her? What kind of stupid remark was that? What party? What date?

Go soak your head, Thelma. How'd you know Polly wasn't here, anyway? See how you like having a snorer share your room with you. Just you see.

I decided to study. I always study when I'm depressed. The phone rang again. What was this, Grand Central Station?

"Yeah?" I said.

"Hi," a lilting voice said. "Are you busy or can you talk?"

"My mother's standing over me with a stopwatch," I said. Well, she would've been if it wasn't for her migraine. "Who's this?"

"It's Nancy, silly."

"Nancy who?"

Nancy's laugh trilled up and down my spine. "Nancy Bishop, that's who. I only sit behind you every day in English class."

That Nancy. Nancy, the high kicker, the would-be Rockette. How come you didn't ask Al for dinner? I felt like saying.

As if she'd read my thoughts, Nancy said, "Al slept over. She's a riot. I really like her. She's precious." She laughed again. I put my finger in my ear.

"Precious?" I said when she stopped laughing. "What does that mean?"

"Oh, you know. She's a riot."

"You said that already."

"She talked about you all the time," Nancy said. "Told me all kinds of things about you. Want to hear what she told me?"

"No," I said. "My mother's getting out the whip. I got to go." I hung up.

What kinds of things had Al told Nancy about me? She had some nerve talking about me to someone she knew as little as she knew Nancy. Why didn't she go back to her kicking and knock herself out?

Teddy came home. I hadn't even realized he was missing. "Where were you?" I asked him.

"At my friend Craig's house," he said.

"Craig? I thought your friend was named Hubie," I said.

"It is. I've got more than one friend, don't forget. I've got Hubie and Craig and Eddie." He ticked them off on his fingers.

"Go wash your hands and face," I told him. See. Even a wimp like Teddy has more than one friend.

This thought depressed me more than I'd thought possible.

Polly got home about five. She took off her shoes and put them under the dining room table. I didn't say anything. She had promised she wouldn't do that. She knew it drove my father bonkers.

"Thelma called," I said in the midst of drinking a glass of water. I hate to drink water, but I was purging my system of poison. I felt as if I were awash with poison. I tried not to look at Polly's shoes.

"What'd she want?" Polly said. She opened the refrigerator door and looked inside. "Anything to eat?"

"Just what you see," I said. "My mother doesn't feel so hot. I said I'd get the dinner. We're having spaghetti. You can make the salad. There's Italian bread, and we can have fruit for dessert."

"I'll make the spaghetti sauce," Polly said.

"It's already made."

"Who made it?" Polly said, surprised.

"Aunt Millie," I said, getting a jar of Aunt Millie's Sauce from the cupboard, opening it and dumping it in the pan in one smooth motion.

Polly looked as if she'd been hit over the head with a cleaver.

"What are you *doing*?" she asked, astounded.

"What's it look like?"

"You mean you're using prepared sauce? You're

not making it from scratch?" I could tell I had offended Polly and was glad.

"It's perfectly good sauce. As good as yours any day." I drove the thrust home. "My father likes it and so do I. It's very good." I avoided her eyes. "You know where we keep the salad greens, and the dressing is in the bottle."

That really got her.

"I've never had bottled dressing before," she said, the way another person might say they'd never tasted shark meat.

"It's great," I said. "It won't kill you. Don't be such a food snob."

She looked at me a minute, then picked up her books. I think her lip was trembling. Maybe she was hurt. I wanted her to be.

"You hurt Al's feelings, you know," I said.

She turned. "How?" she asked.

"When you said that about why didn't she mail her dumb letter. That letter means a lot to her."

"I didn't say 'dumb,' I said 'darn.' Teddy called it dumb. I wouldn't say a letter of Al's was dumb."

" 'Dumb' or 'darn,' what's the difference?"

"There's a lot of difference and you know it. I'm sorry, I didn't mean anything. It's just that I get impatient when people keep saying they're going to do something and don't do it. I didn't mean to hurt Al's feelings. That was a tactless thing to say."

I got out the silver and began to set the table.

"Did you go to Thelma's after school?" I said.

"Yes," Polly said. "We finally finished our project. It turned out pretty well."

"Then how come she called you here if you were at her house?"

"Because I only stayed at her house for a little while. Then I stopped to see a friend of mine who just moved in below us."

OK. Polly had another friend. OK for you, Polly. I lined up the paper napkins as if they'd been made of the finest linen.

"Maybe you should've stayed with Thelma," I said. "While your parents were away, I mean. Instead of us. It probably would've been easier all the way around."

"What's the matter with you?" Polly cried. "What the heck's eating you anyway?"

"Nothing," I said. "It's just that you're always over at Thelma's house."

"I'm not always over at her house. Today's the last time."

"And, Polly, listen."

She waited for what I had to say. Her eyes were very bright. She was still as a statue.

I turned my back and wiped off one of the spoons. Polly listened.

"Do you think you could not snore tonight? It

makes it tough to go to sleep when you snore."

"I don't snore!" Polly shouted.

"Yes, you do," I told her. "Every night."

"Why didn't you say something before this?"

"I thought maybe you just snored once in a while. How was I to know you did it every night?"

"I've only been here three nights," Polly said slowly.

I picked up her shoes and handed them to her. I didn't say anything. She got the message. It was the first time I'd ever seen Polly blush. Her face got as red as Al's sometimes does.

"How about if I sleep on the living room couch?' Polly said. "That way I wouldn't disturb you."

"Oh, my father doesn't like people sleeping on the couch. He wants to sit up and watch television, and he can't if somebody's sleeping there."

"OK, I'll put a pillow over my head," Polly said.

"You might suffocate," I said.

"So I suffocate. There are worse things in the world," she told me. She went into her room. Our room. The room we shared. She didn't even ask me what Thelma wanted when she called. So I didn't tell her.

That night I couldn't get to sleep. Not because Polly was snoring. She wasn't. She only made a couple of little noises, snuffling ones. Maybe she was coming down with a cold. Maybe she was only breathing. Or crying. I was going to turn on the light, then decided not to.

I felt awful. I'd been as mean as a snake. My head ached. I half sat up.

"Polly," I whispered, in case she was asleep. "Are you awake?"

She didn't answer but I still heard the snuffling.

"Polly, I'm sorry," I whispered again. "I'm really sorry. I didn't mean to be such a rat. It's just that I was mad. Not just at you, at everyone. At life."

I waited a second. It felt good, saying I was sorry. It should make Polly feel good too, if I felt good. Why didn't she answer me?

When she didn't say anything, I lay down again and kept waiting for her to snore at me. She didn't.

Finally, when I'd given up and was just dozing off, she said, "What did Thelma want?"

I turned over and put my pillow over my head. But even through it, I could hear Polly going ZZZZZ, ZZZZZ all night long.

chapter nineteen.

On Tuesday morning the atmosphere in our house was so thick I could've cut it up into little chunks and stacked it, like bricks. My father barely nodded at me when I came into the kitchen.

"I've made the coffee," he said. "But I imagine your mother will want tea."

"Does she still have her migraine?" I said.

"She's feeling better. If you can keep Teddy out of her hair and see that he gets off to school, I'd appreciate it." He poured himself a cup of coffee and took it out to the dining room.

I heard Polly say good morning to him. Then she came into the kitchen.

"I'm making some tea for my mother," I said.

"Maybe she'd like some toast. Toast is good for people who don't feel well," Polly said. We didn't look at each other.

"Good idea."

"I'll make it," Polly said. We bustled around, making tea and toast as if we were preparing an eight-course meal.

"I'll take it in to her if you want," Polly said.

"No," I said. "I will." She's my mother, I wanted to say. I didn't. It occurred to me that maybe Polly missed her mother. If we'd been friends I would've said, "Polly, do you miss your mother?" But we weren't so I didn't. Polly wasn't the type to get homesick, but you never know.

I made Teddy go back and rewash his face. He started to fuss and I said sternly, "Better watch it. Dad's not in such a hot mood this morning. If he hears you, he might let you have it." Teddy subsided.

As we were getting our stuff together to go to school, it began to rain. And thunder and lightning. The weather seemed to suit the mood of all of us. My father went in to say good-bye to my mother. When he came out I handed him his umbrella.

"Good-bye, Dad," I said. He nodded and pushed the elevator button. Oh, boy.

"I have soccer practice after school," I said to my mother before I left. "I can cancel if you want. I'll come home and take care of you."

"You're a good child," she said. "But I can manage. By afternoon I should be perfectly all right. You go to your practice." She kissed me. When I straightened up, I saw Polly standing at the door, looking at us.

"I wanted to say good-bye to your mother," she said. "See if there's anything she wanted."

"Oh, Polly dear," my mother said, "you're very thoughtful. I'm fine, feeling much better. Come here and let me give you a kiss."

I made Teddy wear his yellow slicker and matching hat and his rubber boots. It's his favorite outfit, but he likes to pretend he doesn't want to wear it. After he'd put it on, he looked at himself in the mirror for quite a while.

"Come on, wimp," I finally said. "It's time to go." The three of us, Polly, Teddy, and I, went down to the lobby. Teddy's bus was already there. He sloshed out to the curb looking like something straight out of *Captains Courageous*, which is a book by Rudyard Kipling that I read for the first time a couple of months ago. The pavement was so slick and shiny looking it reminded me of dark gray ice. It was still so dark the streetlights were on.

Polly turned her face to me. In the light she looked pale and sad.

I grabbed her and gave her a kiss on each cheek, the way she'd told me the French do. I wanted her to know I was sorry.

"I told you I was sorry last night," I said. "You must not have heard me."

She smiled. "I heard but I wanted you to say it again," she said.

"You're a rat," I told her.

"I figured something was eating you," she said. "Usually when people get mad at each other, it's because something's eating them."

"Yeah," I said.

Polly put on her rain hat. "I better get going," she said.

"I want to ask you something," I said.

"Make it snappy then."

"Do you miss your mother?"

Polly looked surprised.

"Heck, no," she said. "I might if I was staying home with no one but a sitter or Nanny. But staying with you is lots of fun."

I was glad she felt that way. "See you," I said and went out into the rain. I didn't see Al. She must've gone earlier. She ate lunch with Nancy Bishop. I didn't see them doing any neat high kicks.

At soccer practice I didn't score any goals. The coach hollered at me because I made three fouls.

I guess the World Cup team will have to wait.

When I got out on the street, the rain had stopped. On my way home I checked out those little leaves on the trees. They were still hanging in there. Just like me.

132

My mother was in the living room reading when I let myself in. That was a good sign. The migraine must be over. When she had one, she couldn't stand to read.

"You're all right?" I said.

She nodded. The circles under her eyes were dark, but she was smiling.

"Did you and Dad have a fight?" I asked.

"Yes," she said. "How did you know?"

"Because you always have a headache when you fight." I wanted to ask her what they'd fought about, but I figured I'd gone far enough.

"I'm sorry." She sighed. "I wish I could say we hadn't fought. But we did. It's practically impossible to live with someone and not fight. Once in a while, anyway."

"Yeah," I agreed. "It's hard for me to live in the same room with Polly and not fight too. It was different when she only slept over one night. It's just that sometimes she snores and I can't sleep so well."

I shouldn't have said that.

"Polly could change with Teddy," my mother said. "We could put him in with you and she could have his room."

"That's OK," I almost shouted. "It'll be all right. I really love Polly. But you know, it's a small room and she leaves her shoes lying around and I'm afraid that'll make Dad mad and stuff like that."

"I know," my mother said, smiling.

"And then too," I said slowly, "I had a fight with Al on account of she's all worried about whether she gets a letter from this kid named Brian, and also she's jealous because Polly's staying with me, and—I don't know. Everything's a mess."

She nodded. "It's a fact of life that when people are unhappy, for whatever reason, they want to make other people unhappy. So they lash out and make wounds. It isn't nice and it isn't kind, but that's the way it is. The most important thing, I guess, is not to make the wound any deeper than you can. Try not to inflict your own hurts and anger on other people. It's hard not to, I know. But you must try."

"And so must you," I said.

"You're right. So must I."

"Mom, tell me the truth. Is there really any such thing as living happily ever after?" I said.

"If by 'happily ever after' you mean life without any kind of conflict," she said after thinking a moment, "then I guess the answer would have to be no. But happiness doesn't necessarily mean no fighting, either."

"Some people like to fight, I think," I said.

"You're right. They do. And other people hate fighting. It makes them ill."

"I'm sort of in between," I said.

The doorbell rang. Two, then one, then two.

Al. It had to be her.

"Aren't you going to answer it?" my mother asked, looking at me quizzically.

"I'm going," I said. Let her cool her heels. She didn't have to think I was going to fling open the door and act as if nothing had happened.

"Ta-da!" Al cried. Then she did a little belly dance with a couple of bumps and grinds thrown in for good measure.

She waved an envelope in my face.

"You got a letter!" I shouted, forgetting for the moment that we'd had a fight and weren't friends. "You got a letter!" We put our arms around each other and danced up and down in the hall.

"You could have knocked me down with a banana," Al said, stopping at last, red in the face. Maybe it was the exertion or maybe it was the reflection from her outfit. She was dressed all in red: red shirt, red jeans, red sweater. Only her sneakers were green.

"Come on in," I said.

"What goes on?" my mother asked.

"Al got a letter," I explained. "From this kid she met at her father's wedding."

One minute Al was grinning like a butcher's dog. The next she looked sober and sedate and older, somehow.

"Not from *him*," she said scornfully. "From *them*. First," she said, walking around our living room in circles, "first, they're having a barn dance. In their barn."

"Where else?" I said. She didn't hear me.

"Then they're having a fiddler, that's what Louise called it, a fiddler and a caller and everything. I've never been to a barn dance. I expect I can pick it up though. And corn on the cob and hamburgers and homemade ice cream. I've never had homemade ice cream. I imagine it's a lot different from the stuff you get around here," she said, very serious. "A lot different."

She was miles away, eating homemade ice cream and listening to a genuine fiddler play his tunes that she was dancing to in a real barn.

"They want me to stay a month," Al said. "I told them my mother might get lonely. I'd have to see. I'll have to talk it over with her. Boy, will my mother be glad I got a letter. I've been some pain in the neck around our house, I bet. My mother is really a very patient woman. I'll have to see what she wants to do about our cruise. But first let me read parts of Louise's letter to you."

Try and stop her. My mother and I sat down and waited.

"Louise starts off by saying 'I would have telephoned you, but I myself like to get an invitation in writing. That way, if you like, you can paste it in your scrapbook.'"

Al looked at us both. "Can you imagine her being

that thoughtful? I don't even have a scrapbook. I'm going to go right out and buy one, though. It's essential. I don't know why I didn't think of a scrapbook before this." She shook her head in amazement at herself.

"And when you think about it, what she says is very true. A written invitation is much nicer. That way you never forget. It's very true."

My mother and I didn't say anything. It wasn't necessary.

" 'The boys have already begun to get your room ready,' " Al read to us. " 'They've decorated it with hay and Sam wanted to put a box of fireflies under your bed. I told him by the time you got here, they'd be dead. So he's holding off. But if you see a strange light in the middle of the night, you'll know what causes it.' "

Al laughed. "That Sam," she said. "He's a hot ticket." She read more of the letter to us, tasting each word as it came out of her mouth. Finally she put the letter in her pocket.

"I'm sorry," she said to my mother. "You probably have stuff to do. It's just that I waited so long to hear. I thought they'd forgotten. Now it's all right. They really do want me." A look of wonder was on her face.

"They really do."

My mother hugged Al. "Of course they do," she said. "Who wouldn't?"

My mother has a wonderful way with words sometimes. This was one of those times.

The bell rang again. It was Polly.

"Al got a letter," I said.

Polly clapped her hands. "Terrific!" she said.
"What's he say?"

"He?" Al said.

"Yeah, the kid you met at the wedding," Polly
said. "What's he got to say for himself?"

My mother leaped into the breach.

"Al's been invited to a barn dance at her father's
place. They're having a fiddler and homemade ice
cream," she said. "Tell Polly about it, Al."

The light on Al's face dimmed.

"Oh, it's not so much," she said. "It's just a letter
from Louise."

"Terrific!" Polly said. "I want you to tell me what
she said. Everything. I'll be back in a sec. I have to go
to the bathroom. Don't say a word until I get back. I
don't want to miss anything."

After Polly left, Al said to me, "I mailed it."

"You did?"

She nodded. "After I got mad at you I went right
home and mailed the letter to him. What the heck do
I care if he answers?"

"Right," I said. "That's the spirit." But my heart
sank.

"I won one out of two and that ain't bad, baby," Al
said.

138

"Right," I said again.

"Did I read you the part about the box of fireflies Sam put under my bed?" Al said.

"Yes," I said.

Al grabbed my arm and pinched me.

"He doesn't have to answer," she whispered fiercely. "He doesn't have to. But he better. He just better."

"He will," I told her.

Her face collapsed.

"No," she said. "You don't believe that and neither do I." Polly came back then and I didn't have to answer.

Which was good.

chapter twenty.

"So I said to Vi," Al said on our way home next day, "I said, 'Vi, I won't stay with them for more than three weeks. I don't want you to get lonely.' I told you Dad and Louise and the boys want me to stay for a whole month, didn't I?" she asked.

I nodded.

"Do you really call your mother Vi to her face?" I asked.

"No," Al answered. "I don't think she's ready for that yet. My mother is a curious mixture of modern and old-fashioned. She demands respect. She wouldn't like it if I called her Vi. But it's OK if I do it behind her back. Then you know what she said?"

140

I shook my head. Sometimes I remind myself of a puppet. Pull the strings and I do what's expected of me. Al was out of the pits now and on top of the world. Good. The postal service had kicked through and brought her one of the letters she'd been waiting for. But how about when she was down? How about how she acted then?

"She said she'd make plans to go on the cruise without me. I said who would she go with, and she said maybe with Mr. Wright. Separate cabins, of course," Al said, baring her teeth at me.

"No kidding." I tried to imagine my mother going on a cruise with somebody. I couldn't. Especially not with my father. I could see him, pacing around the ship, playing shuffleboard, maybe a little bridge. I understand people on cruises play a lot of both. My father would climb the walls he'd be so itchy.

"I was amazed," Al went on. "My mother's really quite a person."

"Yes," I agreed, "she is."

"So's yours," Al said generously.

"You know something?" I said.

"What?" The sun was shining smack into Al's glasses, so I couldn't tell what was going on inside her head.

"You're pretty tough to be around when things aren't going right for you. Do you know that?"

I could feel her stiffen.

I laughed but it turned out phony and hollow

sounding, the kind of sound people make when what they're saying isn't really all that funny. It isn't funny at all.

"It's all right now because you got your invite from Louise and that's great. But for a while there I thought maybe you were going to be just another Rockette. You know what I mean?"

Al took off her glasses and wiped them on her shirt.

"You're like that too," she said slowly.

"I am not," I said indignantly.

"Yes, you are. You can be just as snotty as I can."

I opened my mouth to say she was crazy. Then I shut it. I guess she was right. I wish she wasn't. I'd been terrible to Polly. I know that.

"My mother says that when people are unhappy they want to make other people unhappy," I said. "We were having a discussion about fighting, people fighting with each other." I didn't tell Al about my mother and father fighting. I didn't want her to know. She thought my mother and father were just about perfect. Let her think so.

"She said to try not to inflict your own hurt and anger on other people. She said it wasn't easy but we should try."

Al nodded. "Your mother is a wise woman, O Skinny One. A very wise woman. Sometimes when my mother's had a bad day at the store, she comes home and gives me a hard time for not putting the top on the toothpaste or something silly like that.

142

And I bet when Mr. Keogh blows his top the way he did the other day, it was probably because the principal gave him heat or maybe his wife gave him liver for dinner. But it seems to me," Al said, still polishing her glasses, "it seems to me if you're friends, you have to take the bitter with the sweet. Grin and bear it is what I say." She frowned at me. "One thing. You didn't have to call me big and fat. I've lost four pounds this month. At the rate I'm going I might even be svelte when I go to the farm."

"You're not big and fat," I said. I felt great now. "You're thin as a wand. When you turn sideways, I can hardly see you."

"Yeah, I'm thin as a wand," Al said, putting on her glasses, "and just as shapeless." We got a good laugh out of that.

"One thing," I said. "We should make a pact not to get mad at each other. At least not unless we have a very good reason."

"It's not the worst thing in the world—getting mad, I mean," Al said. "If only I could figure out some way to get mad and not say anything mean until I got over being mad. It's the things people say to each other when they're mad that cause trouble."

"You have a point," I told her.

"You know, it's a funny thing," Al said. "You may not know it, but yesterday I was jealous of Polly. Her staying with you for so long, sharing your room like you were sisters and everything. But now that I know

I'm going, really going, to visit Louise and my father and the boys at the farm, I'm not jealous of her any more. I must be a very small person to be jealous of a nice girl like Polly.

"It's not always easy, being a friend," she said.

"Nothing worth having is easy," I said.

Al looked impressed. "You sound just like your mother," she told me.

chapter twenty-one.

My mother and father are throwing a dinner party Friday night. Polly's chef, Al and I are waitresses, and Teddy is, pardon the expression, the butler. This last fact in itself is enough to make this dinner party memorable.

Teddy wakes up saying, "Who shall I say is calling?" and goes to sleep saying the same. Al is driving me crazy. All day she mutters, "Serve from the left, take away from the right." Then she comes to a grinding halt and says, "Or is it the other way around? Serve from the right, take away from the left. Oh, my gosh, I'll never get it straight. I'll louse up everything."

"Just watch the soup," I told her. "Be careful you don't spill the soup down some woman's front."

"Soup?" Al sounded panicky. "Are we having soup? I hadn't counted on soup. That might be hairy. Soup. Oh, my gosh, soup."

"I'll tell Polly to scratch the soup," I said. "Calm down."

"What kind of soup was she planning on?" Al said, not hearing me. "I hope it isn't noodle soup. That could be disaster."

We've discussed the menu a thousand times. Polly has a shopping list that would choke a horse.

My mother is having second thoughts about the whole thing. My father says he wouldn't be at all surprised if several of the guests sneak out to the kitchen after the dinner and try to lure Polly away at a much higher salary. He's just trying to introduce a little levity into the proceedings and getting nowhere. Things are getting tenser and tenser.

The day of the party Al and I went straight home from school. She kept up the "serve from the left" routine until I was ready to strangle her. When we got off at our floor, I saw mail on the table. It must've come after Al's mother went to work.

"Well, anyway," I said, to soothe her, "that's one thing you don't have to sweat out any more. A letter You got your letter."

I opened our front door. "See you," I said.

Al screamed. That scream actually did curdle my

146

blood. I could feel it curdling. I ran halfway down the hall. She was as green as a cucumber. Then she turned red. It crossed my mind that if she was going to be sick, that would leave me to wait on table all alone. I wasn't sure I could handle that.

"Look at this!" Al shouted. I had to grab her arm to make her stop flapping the postcard in my face. It was a picture of sailboats on Lake Michigan in Chicago.

"Read it," she commanded.

It said: "Hear I am in the Windy City with my 4H Club. Here you're coming for a visit. I'll meet you with a brass band. Ha Ha. Your friend Brian."

"Boy," I said, "Mr. Keogh would flip over this kid's spelling."

"He's a terrible speller, isn't he?" Al said joyfully.

I hope after she gets to know him she still thinks Brian's perfect. It occurred to me it must be a burden living up to being perfect.

Al screamed again.

"Will you stop that? You're hurting my eardrums," I said. She handed me an envelope. It was her letter to Brian with her return address on the back. Someone had stamped "Returned for Insufficient Postage" on it in red letters.

"He never got it," Al said slowly. "He didn't know I wrote to him. He sent me a postcard on his own. He never knew I wrote to him at all. He wrote first!"

So much for ERA.

She grabbed me and started dancing up and down the hall.

"My cup runneth over!" she shouted.

The door of our apartment opened. Teddy stuck out his head. His hair always looks slightly moth-eaten. "Who shall I say is calling?" he inquired.

"Whom shall I say is calling," Al corrected Teddy.

"That's right." Teddy nodded. "I have to practice to get it right. Who shall I say is calling? Then I have to take the guests' hats and coats and dump 'em on the bed. It's a big responsibility."

We went inside to see what there was to eat.

"Al got a postcard from Brian," I told my mother.

"That's nice," she said, wielding the ammonia bottle wildly, not really caring. "If you girls haven't anything better to do, I've got a couple of things that need doing."

I dragged Al toward the kitchen. "In a sec," I said. "We're starving." Al kept walking around in circles, reading her postcard and reciting, "Serve from the right, take away from the left. No, no, that's not right, it's the other way around."

I got us each an apple, then turned her in the direction of the door and followed.

"Who shall I say is calling?" Teddy shouted after us.

"Get me some rags, somebody!" my mother shouted. I rang for the elevator. I felt the need of some fresh air.

148

"You coming?" I asked Al.

"No," she said. "I have to read my mail." She did a combination of a belly dance and a burlesque queen's gyrations. "Hey!" she hissed from her open door. "Listen, thanks."

"For what?"

"You know." She waved vaguely. "For being a help. For listening to me. I know I was a pest, always crying on your shoulder, telling you my troubles. I know it, but I couldn't help it. But anyway, thanks a lot."

"That's OK," I said. The elevator stopped at our floor.

"If you ever need any advice, you know, about what to do if you don't get a letter, call on me. I may not know all the answers," she said modestly, "but I can sure phony up a couple. You're a real pal," she said.

"Your old pal, Al," I said.

She looked surprised. "Well put," she said. "That's exactly right. That's what you are, my old pal."

We smiled at each other. Then I got on the elevator and she went inside her apartment, closing the door softly.

MS READ-a-thon—
a simple way to start youngsters reading

Boys and girls between 6 and 14 can join the MS READ-a-thon and help find a cure for Multiple Sclerosis by reading books. And they get two rewards — the enjoyment of reading, and the great feeling that comes from helping others.

Parents and educators: For complete information call your local MS chapter. Or mail the coupon below.

Kids can help, too!

Mail to:
National Multiple Sclerosis Society
205 East 42nd Street
New York, N.Y. 10017
I would like more information about the MS READ-a-thon and how it can work in my area.

MS Mystery Sleuth™

Name_____
(please print)
Address_____
City_____ State_____ Zip_____
Organization_____

1—80